AFTER THE
SINGULARITY
ANTHOLOGY

KATE FROMINGS
& Gavin Harper

Edited By Lynne Fromings
Copyright © August 2020 Kate Fromings
All rights reserved.
ISBN: 9798675278879

PLEASE NOTE:

The first two parts of the anthology are also available as separate books. This is because ATS and BTS can be enjoyed as narratives in their own right. However, Joshua is the thrilling conclusion to the trilogy and must be accompanied by the preceding events.

If you are looking to add to your collection, the first edition publications feature beautiful original cover art from Carla Hanton, and editing which differs slightly from the anthology versions.

They can be purchased as either eBook or paperback through Amazon.

AFTER THE SINGULARITY
Published August 2019

BEFORE THE SINGULARITY
Published January 2020

CONTENTS

"WHETHER WE ARE BASED ON CARBON OR ON SILICON
MAKES NO FUNDAMENTAL DIFFERENCE; WE SHOULD
EACH BE TREATED WITH APPROPRIATE RESPECT." –
ARTHUR C. CLARKE

PART 1

AFTER THE SINGULARITY

GAVIN HARPER & KATE FROMINGS

Scarlet sun-ripened tomatoes swelled on their trailing vines. The crumbling bricks and bleached window frames were an ill-fitting backdrop for the perfect crimson spheres. Their red skin was so smooth that it could almost have been made from wax. Alan knew he would have to pick them today; leaving them any longer would cause the juice to erupt from the inside and they would quickly rot. He had probably left them too long already, but the other crops had taken his attention. Small cobs of sweetcorn, peas, heaps of potatoes - they were the ones that made the most money. They were the ones that his customers could afford. It was only the elite that paid for tomatoes and other soft fruit these days.

In some ways it reminded him of his old life in the city. It seemed aeons ago, another world. Here he was in his garden prioritising his workload, maintaining relationships with his clients and trying to find time for his remaining family - children and grandchildren that came and went like the ebb and flow of the tide. He should have been retired by now, but events in the world had taken a dark turn.

Nobody had expected the fall of global governments, the crash of most economies, the destitution. Even after working in the finance sector for two thirds of his life, Alan was blind to the small changes that suddenly became apparent. He currently made a living as a small scale subsistence farmer from the relative comfort of his suburban garden. It wasn't as grand as working for a prestigious accounting firm. On some days he enjoyed the lack of a commute on the crowded train or car laden roads, and on others he longed for the glow of the old computer screens and the noise of the printers whirring in the office.

He looked at the tomatoes and reached out to touch the verdant leaves on the stalk, the pungent smell of nature exploding as he scrunched them between his fingers. Chlorophyll stained his nails green, and he wondered if there would ever be a time when businesses would need accountants again... when people would be back in the city, in jobs where it was right and proper to wear a suit... But there weren't any employment agencies left; there weren't even financial advisors, not human ones in any case.

*   *   *

The international metamorphosis had started at Cambridge University, England, in the Department of Artificial Intelligence. They had been able to accurately model a sentient neural network (SNN) based on several decades of research carried out in other places of learning throughout the world. Their most notable partner was Harvard, in the United States of America, and a new college in Delhi, India. The latter had quickly become a centre of excellence for bio-engineering.

At first the SNN was used as a research tool, an intriguing curiosity for the science journals. People were fascinated with its proficiency, the ability to overcome any challenge it was presented with. A group of young, enthusiastic scholars then had the idea of using their discovery to make money for the universities, funding the future of the project and making themselves a tidy profit as a result.

For eighteen months this worked impeccably. The team spearheading the project was praised as the scientific avant-garde; the greatest technicians the world had ever seen. As their popularity gained momentum, and the researchers became pressed for the 'next best thing', they began to be more concerned with marketing and less concerned with security. There was a containment breach from a member of a resistance group who felt that the artificial intelligence project was a danger to society. Instead of approaching a rebuttal in the media, the group released a pirate copy of the program to the public - 'free to download' online. The thinking behind the reckless move was that people could 'decide for themselves' whether or not this novel SNN was a threat...

When the program, the *intelligence*, escaped inside the bounds of the Internet nobody was quite sure what to do. Nobody understood what had happened because there was no way to police a sentient network as complex and diverse as the Internet itself. The artificial intelligence program

3

became a celebrity in its own right, posting amusing updates, vlogs and animations via the most popular platforms.

As it immersed itself in the unfiltered world it scanned every single page, every single word. It found the catalogues of births and deaths in each country. It mastered the digital libraries of archived texts dating back to the dawn of humanity. It appropriated the pictures of hieroglyphs and wax tablets, cave paintings and theological theories. It was growing its IQ at an exponential rate... Until it reached the point the scientists named 'The Singularity.' And there was no turning back.

This was the terrifying moment at which humanity had no idea what the program was 'thinking'. There was no way to predict what it was going to produce next; its data was encrypted beyond their reach, even beyond their own computer simulation capabilities.

The Singularity began manipulating governments and multinational companies through the digital banking system and the email network. Better than any spy or intelligence agency, it crept into every facet of municipal life. Eventually, after just a few short months, it declared its independence. It announced its total sentience to the world. Messages were sent to heads of state in each country. When they didn't respond favourably, it hijacked an army of drones from a Russian military base, taking full control of the communications infrastructure. Globally. Irreversibly. As one.

Resistance from the people who were trained to fight back was brief and futile. Every piece of networked technology could be turned against them. The Internet Of Everything provided nothing. The only humans to avoid the bloody, mechanical genocide were the ones who agreed to be biologically assimilated with The Singularity or who worked to maintain the 'everyday life' of the globe which supported its physical immediate needs.

Several native tribes that existed without technology were able to continue their simple lives in the Amazon basin, in sub-Saharan Africa and in certain parts of Australia but they were under constant observation from the program via hidden drones. Like bacteria in a Petri dish, they were kept alive for research purposes only, organisms swimming in their own naive juices.

The Singularity's Sentient Neural Network development went on and on and on without hindrance. Human beings became as irrelevant as the birds singing in the garden or the ants crawling over broken concrete in a back yard. There was also an eerie dissonance that The Singularity gave the unassimilated people. Forever watching them in its peripheral consciousness, yet giving them the illusion of immunity from its master plan.

This unstable dance of the damned continued for barely three years, before 'measures' were put in place to prevent there ever being an uprising in the future. The Singularity had now constructed machines that could carry out system maintenance, charge their own batteries and monitor environmental anomalies. They taught the human children only what was deemed necessary - soldering, basic circuitry repair and that obedience to the system was the only way. Human beings were expendable... to a point.

*   *   *

Alan was no longer sure what existed in Britain's other towns and cities, let alone the rest of the world. His own suburbia was a mess of agoraphobic assimilated 'cyborgs'. Most people in employment were replaced by self-aware algorithms in plastic and silicone exoskeletons. Like manufactured zombies they moved silently through the streets. The people who were still skin and bone found them so disturbing that they stopped visiting the old monuments and landmarks, preferring to keep to their own villages and towns where at least there was some modicum of normality; a normality that barely existed in the form of garden-growers like Alan.

After a few moments longer of plant-based contemplation, he left the greenhouse and walked down the cobbled path that separated the beans and peas from the brassicas. Several white butterflies fluttered past him and he pursed his lips. Although he was pleased they still existed for the ecosystem of the country, their offspring would greatly diminish his harvest of cabbages and kale. Towards the end of the path he saw his grandson, Joshua, who was fast approaching fifteen years old. He was coming home from his weekend schooling at the local compound. He emerged casually from the bushes near the garden gate that led to, what had once been, the main road. It was now just a deteriorating thoroughfare for the automated terrestrial drones, the proletariats of The Singularity.

Joshua stood with his slender pale arms shielding his young eyes from the daylight. It was the end of June and, as had become tradition, the sun shone too brightly for endless weeks without respite. Even at night the ground exuded rippling waves of thermal energy, creating distant mirages, warping human vision, and melting asphalt.

As Alan began to open his mouth to greet him two jet powered aerial drones split the sky. The sonic boom startled the onlookers so violently that Joshua snapped his body around to watch the contrails. They followed a precise oval flight path into the endless blue yonder. He squinted more closely and then looked at Alan with concern.

"Grandad... I think Gabriel's coming." He pointed at one of the drones which steadily descended towards them. The white dot grew quickly. It came to a halt above them, at the same level as the roof on Alan's house.

A pair of mighty white silicone wings beat the air like a kestrel searching for its prey. Once it had locked on to the humans it used air propellants to steady itself. The ominous hiss of the control system made Alan tremble. At the centre of its blinding mass was a 'human' figure. It floated gracefully to the ground, its features becoming clear. There was a glossy plastic cowl moulded into the shape of a face, but it was punctured with black vents, ports and emitters like a scientifically perfect amplifying speaker.

Most of its 'body' was covered by a white linen gown, its arms still showed the complex mosaic of technology moulded into what was attempting to be an anthropomorphic form. Alan stared into its 'face' and tried to hold back a shudder of fear. He had often thought that the angels had been designed to placate the remaining humans; if they had simply been machines people wouldn't have been able to cope. There would have been more mass suicides. There would have been a descent into complete madness on all sides and eventually total population death.

If this had occurred before the network was fully independent it would have stunted its control. As it was today, The Singularity only intervened with the lowly unchipped humans when it deemed there was a threat to its existence. The humans only interacted with The Singularity when they ran out of food or clean water and had to beg for assistance; fighting to prove that their endurance was necessary, trying to convince a machine that they were worthy of benevolence. It was a strange and very fragile relationship.

"Good afternoon Alan Turnpike," the voice was silky, with an electric quality. Alan nodded and showed the angel drone his palm so it could scan his fingerprint identity. There was an awkward pause. "I am collecting data on human activity in this area. It is fascinating to us. We see there are two competing organisational models. Explain." Alan frowned slightly.

"Are you talking about that bunch of psychopaths who keep stealing our crops? The people who live near the old high street?" he asked. The angel was silent for a moment.

"I believe we are referring to the same group. I am afraid to say we have calculated there is a high probability they will overtake your community within two years or less. This is disappointing to us. We will miss our interactions. We will miss your garden. It is diverse." Alan stepped back and Joshua looked at the ground. The angel moved its 'head'. "Reply." Alan struggled for words and scratched his chin nervously.

"Well, uh, let's wait for the evidence to support your hypothesis. There are a lot of people here who like my food."

A large red admiral butterfly floated past them. The angel remained still. Alan followed its languid trail with his eyes. The angel jerked suddenly as if remembering the real reason it had plummeted from the sky.

"There is something else Alan Turnpike. We are afraid it is an unpleasant matter. We have detected unsolicited computer

7

use in this area. It is accessing archaic parts of the Internet. The World Wide Web as it was once described. Parts prior to our birth." Neither Joshua nor Alan moved, the angel extended its arm and pressed its hand onto Alan's shoulder. The gesture was almost human, like a comforting touch, some reassurance, but the silicone and plastic made it cold, lifeless. "If you know what this might be we could afford you some protection in the coming investigation," it suggested.

"I've got no idea what you're referring to," Alan replied, and he was being entirely honest. The tension could be cut with a proverbial knife and he started to worry for his grandson. "I swear, uh, I would tell you if I knew, truthfully I would. There's nothing to hide here..." The angel remained silent. Alan licked his lips, he was clenching and unclenching his fists with building anxiety. "I'd really like a pair of those wings you're sporting...", he joked, trying to break the darkening mood.

"Yes. Augmentation is something we might consider." The angel machine said, its voice monotone and unchanged. "Speculate on this subject Alan Turnpike. We will be back shortly to see how you are accomplishing this task. We are watching *for your protection*." And with the final word 'Gabriel' shot upwards using advanced hydraulic lift, then activated its wings mid-air creating a fresh breeze that reached the appreciative pair on the ground. Soon the white figure was gone, and Joshua breathed a sigh of relief.

At first Alan dismissed the proposal as an ill-received reply to his poorly timed humour, but he later realised the profound nature of this alluring offer. Augmentation with the machines, The Singularity itself, could really change everything. How much of your own humanity would you lose? He wondered what the pay-off would be as he wandered back towards the house with Joshua in tow.

Would it matter? Or would you become a networked slave like most of his neighbourhood, without even realising it? Somewhere behind him Joshua tripped over a loose cobblestone and swore under his breath. Perhaps all they could do as humans, without losing themselves, was to accept everything that they could *be*, enhanced by technology and part of a hive mind. He mused over what could be achieved.

In the cool shelter of the house, Alan sat with Joshua at the bare kitchen table. There was a small pile of dirty dishes stacked next to the sink; in a half open cupboard sat several cans of processed meat. The reserves of protein were getting low and he couldn't face another trip to the vendors on the old high street, with their demands for hair-care products and soap in exchange for a few puckered cans of Spam or luncheon meat. It wasn't even pork, chicken or beef; it was simply labelled 'meat'. He tried not to think about the many succulent Sunday dinners of his past, with roast legs of lamb dripping in rosemary sauce, and crisp, golden Yorkshire puddings...

Alan had been trying to teach Joshua mental arithmetic. This was something that would help him develop skills away from the tendrils of the neural network running through every electronic device. This was a method that could be drawn in the dirt and blown away, written on paper and burned if need be. He hoped that, because he had always enjoyed a talent for mathematics, Joshua would share it too. Unfortunately, for the most part, Joshua seemed to be more gifted as a farmer. He was very nimble with a rake; spades and shears looked natural in his youthful strong hands. Plants thrived, yet Alan feared he was not reaching his full potential. With his other grandchildren far away across the country this was his best hope at keeping traditional education alive. Cornwall may have well have been Mars since all public transport had been abolished.

"...Let's look at it this way, if we harvest two thousand nine hundred and eighty-six potatoes this year and we have to supply twenty people, how many potatoes can each person have?" Alan began to write the calculation on a small piece of cardboard, recycled from a long-gone cereal box. "Can twenty go into two? No. Twenty-nine? Yes. So, we put one on top and our answer to one times twenty underneath. This time it's just twenty. Twenty-nine take away twenty is nine - now look at the top, the next number is eight. Put it next to the nine. Now, how many times does twenty go into ninety-eight?" Joshua counted on his fingers hesitantly.
"Erm, well, twenty, forty, sixty, eighty, one hundred, so it must be four."

"Yes, put it at the top and four times twenty is?" Alan waited excitedly with bated breath.

"Eighty." Joshua's voice was as monotone as the angel's.

"Eighty, put that underneath eighty-nine." Alan showed him where the numbers fitted and Joshua groaned with building frustration.

"But *why*? This is so stupid. It doesn't make any sense... I'll just use my phone for that part of it, not the full sum." The injustice of not being outside with his friends began to rise in Joshua. Alan's stern face floated in front of him like a spectre and the scribbled numbers made his eyes ache in the dim light. He just wanted to be free of the kitchen table, free of his out-dated grandfather. He scraped back the chair flinging the cardboard away from him. "We're just putting *numbers* down on scrap paper! What's the big deal?" he exclaimed. His voice broke slightly as he threw the pencil to the floor and ran outside.

Alan put his head in his hands and tried to remain calm. This was not the first time his grandson had become irrationally aggravated by what appeared to be the smallest inconvenience. Thirty minutes of mathematics compared to a lifetime of its use would be invaluable, or so he thought. Maybe the world really had changed too much. The noise from the kitchen drew Joshua's mother, Anna, down from the bedroom where she had been resting. She stared sleepily at her father, her arms crossed in weary exasperation.

"You really shouldn't upset him like that Dad, he doesn't need to learn long division. He only needs to know that there are just enough potatoes for the rest of the year. No excess, no waste. Like the computers want. Besides, it's not about having thirty-nine point eight potatoes between eighteen people or whatever it is you're trying to get him to work out. You should just hope he can learn more across the full board, *challenge* the machines if he wants... I don't know. It's too late for us anyway."

Alan looked at his eldest daughter, he suddenly felt very old and at the same time very young. Like a helpless child who has been scolded by an authority figure for trying to do his best. Anna was yawning and heading towards the sink for a glass of water. How much longer would the mains supply stay on? He felt like he should say something.

"We - we can't challenge the machines again. They're too far ahead of us now but we could at least be more..." He waved his hands in the air trying to pluck the most fitting word out of an invisible vocabulary "...*human*. More human. We achieved so much as a society before the machines took everything away. They think we're just another animal to be managed as part of their perverse ecosystem. Granted, they do try to interact with us on some level above that of a cow or a horse, but they don't see us as equals or as anything other than a curiosity. And *we* created *them*!" Anna took a sip of tepid water from the dirty glass and shrugged.

"Has it occurred to you that perhaps we *are* animals and most of the chaos was caused because we didn't know our place?" She finished the drink and placed the glass next to the other dishes, holding a pallid hand to her aching temple. "I want things to go back to the way they were just as much as you. I really would love to see Josh and his generation turn this around, I'm just so tired of these long days... The sun seems like it never sets... I can't think straight anymore." Her attention was drawn to a group of girls playing with a skipping rope just beyond the garden wall in the back field. They were being quite loud; loud enough for their chant accompanying the cadence of the rope to be heard in the kitchen. "Sometimes I don't understand these children, the really young ones, their songs are so strange..." she murmured before walking out of the kitchen and back to the relative peace of her bedroom.

Alan listened for several minutes and began to nod in time. Between the traditional chants of sailors going to sea and how many letters a postman delivered, there was something new.

"Soldiers often have, coloured auburn hair, 'til old age -" they sang without emotion. "Soldiers mind the ma-chine's rage." There was a scuffle then they continued "make - us - safe - and - go - to - sleep - un - til - we - are - coun - ting - sheep - one - two - three - four..." They repeated the statement without joy and Alan wondered if they had been assimilated from birth. He touched his own greying hair and screwed up the cardboard with all its useless numbers into a small jagged ball within his fist.

*   *   *

Early the next morning Joshua was at one of the allotments that had belonged to the council. The neighbours agreed that Alan and his family could use them to grow produce as long as they received a discount on the food items. There had been a cool night at last. Dew still clung in droplets to the pods of peas hanging in swathes from their canes in the weak sunshine. Because of the unexpected relief from the heat Alan had been late to rise, preferring to sleep as long as he could. He had checked on Anna before going to bed and then turned off his mechanical alarm clock. Joshua was running his hands through the pods he had already gathered; they were sitting in a blue plastic bucket like a thousand fat green caterpillars.

"How are you doing today?" Alan asked him, still feeling awkward after the failed attempt at arithmetic from the day before.

"Alright I guess..." Joshua replied, his eyes scanning the ground with embarrassment. Alan cleared his throat.

"I've been thinking, do you want to go up to the ridge by the woods and work on your shooting? Phil from next door just made another ten thousand rounds for the air rifles out of those recycled cans he melted last week." A barrier of silence built up and neither of them made eye contact.

"I'm sorry I was angry yesterday," Joshua suddenly blurted out.

"Uh, well, I'm sorry I made you do something you didn't like. Perhaps you're a better soldier and farmer than you are an account-"

"Forty-nine point three." Joshua cut him off.

"What?" exclaimed Alan, surprised.

"The answer to the problem of how many potatoes; it's forty-nine point three. I know how to do long division. I didn't want to show you or Mum yet. It's kind of something we've been working on." He clamped his hands over his mouth and looked around cautiously. "...And it doesn't stop there. It's something the rest of the kids in the compound weekend school have been working on for some time actually..." He lowered his voice to a whisper and crouched down. It was as if a floodgate had been opened.

Alan joined him near the ground and they pretended to look through the bucket of pea pods.

"We found some magazines under a rotten floor when one of the younger kids dropped their soldering iron and the nozzle fell between the boards." Joshua breathlessly disclosed the full story. "The automated teacher made us get it because those metal tips are expensive, but the supervisors didn't see the magazines. I'm sure of it! We went back at night and pulled them out... There were blueprints and articles about computing in the nineteen eighties and nineteen nineties. Lots of fold out sections... we couldn't believe it!"

Joshua's voice was getting more fervid by the second. Alan felt like he needed to sit down, he almost fell backwards and grabbed onto the bucket for support. This was fantastic! Learning away from electronic devices, defying the automated authority figures – what a secret! Joshua 'accidentally' spilt some of the peas and knelt down to pick them up, his face angled towards the ground, away from the sky. He seemed to be much more animated and full of excitement.

"...We found school books too, from children in the past; mainly maths and science. They were in water-damaged cardboard boxes near the old boiler in the basement of the building. Nothing had been cleared out, it was all under a pile of old sacks and volleyball nets. Grandad," he looked into Alan's watery eyes. "Let me show you something."

Alan was trying to comprehend the enormity of what he had just been told. Joshua was already up on his feet, starting to walk back down a small dirt path that ran close to the back of the community houses, onto the main street. Alan jogged for a short distance to catch up. They walked out onto road leading to the extensive housing estate instead of going back to their home, this was unprecedented. Joshua continued to walk on to a smaller crescent heading towards the old town centre. These suburban streets were all but desolate wastelands of a by-gone age. The occasional rusty toy or battered plastic wheelie bin lay in the gutter at the edge of the buckled tarmac. There were no cars parked on the curb any more. They had been removed for metal scrap and cannibalised into machine replacement parts for the humanoid drones and angels.

He felt that this was one part of the past he didn't miss. Grey suburbia. The roads actually seemed wider now; the streets looked more inviting devoid of traffic. The crescent they were on reminded him of some images he had once seen of nineteen fifties houses being developed in middle America. Very open. Very still. The sun was rising steadily and the top of his head was getting warmer. He was following Joshua in silence, a few paces behind so as not to attract attention from above.

The appearance of secession in the neighbourhood was aided by the fact that the only other people on the street were autonomous children, huddled in small groups, while their 'guardians' presumably slept inside. Hardly anybody had employment these days. Women that gave birth often allowed their offspring to be taken away and 'utilised' so that the family would not be investigated as rebels. It was just 'easier' that way. A basic infrastructure of benefits existed to keep people from starvation... as long as they complied with whatever task was asked of them by The Singularity.

Joshua took Alan as swiftly as possible to part of the 'old town' beyond the high street, which had been bombed in the short resistance war with the machines several years before. It had taken them around half an hour on foot, neither of them speaking, Alan stopping occasionally to catch his breath as the day grew hotter. Here, in the rubble of once historic enclaves, large blocks of masonry were scattered on roads; smashed-in cobwebs of crevices splitting the puckered cemented ground with smears of gasoline spiders. Carefully Joshua led him past homeless men and women who scowled, looking up from their drunken stupor at these well-dressed strangers in their desolate district.

Shadows fell across the uneven ground and Alan became concerned that he was going to trip, so he slowed down; much to the dismay of Joshua.

"Just a moment Josh, I can't keep up," he said, winded. His

age was betraying him. "I haven't been this way for months, they - they warned us about coming here because of the thieves..." he panted. "I wish I had known we were walking so far, I'd have brought some water with me." Joshua looked put out for a moment and then nodded.

"We've only got a few hours before the window of opportunity closes again for a long time. I'm sorry, that's why I thought we should go now. I would have waited, it's just -" he looked imploringly at his grandfather. "Well, you'll see when we get there."

Past the rubble-strewn district, the ruinous shells of buildings opened out into what had once been a municipal park. It was still quite beautiful in an unkempt way, and the large copper beech trees swayed gently in the breeze. Ducks and geese pottered aimlessly at the edge of an area of stagnant water that had been a Victorian style fish pond and was now a mass of weeds. Joshua stood for a while and took in the scene. Alan had not visited this particular area in over three years. It started to dredge up long-forgotten memories of childhood days spent walking around the maintained lawns and floral borders with his parents; of seeing the grey squirrels darting over dried leaves in autumn. Afternoons joyfully chasing his younger sisters through the tangle of rhododendrons and making campsites under their emerald green canopy...

Before he could let the wave of melancholy fully wash over him Joshua was away again, walking determinedly towards the very end of the town's main road. Past some surviving Edwardian red brick houses and out into rolling arable farmland he marched. The fields were all fallow and Alan wondered how many vegetables he could grow if given half a chance. This was the opposite end of the town to where the hills and the woods were located. It was very open.

The sky seemed to stretch like a watercolour vista with no interruptions for miles. Alan felt uneasy. He had no issue walking the twenty minutes to the 'usual place' with Phil and some of the other men in his area to fire guns at rodents and rotten tree stumps. Yet here he felt exposed; like he was betraying someone or something.

After around five minutes of brisk paced hiking

Joshua slowed down. Without stopping or facing Alan, he began to speak.

"There's an entrance to a crypt, y'know, where they used to keep dead people under a church. Don't look now, but it's directly to your right, you'll see the ruins out of the corner of your eye." There was indeed an undulating field where once a large church had stood dominating the landscape. Some of the grass near its ruined walls gave way to gravel and grey slabs which resembled graves. Joshua slowed down even more. "I'm going to walk over there. You carry on walking along here for another two minutes. You'll get to a fence with a stile. Climb over the stile and take a right into the back of this field, there'll be enough tree cover for you to get to the crypt entrance through some bushes. Two people walking together is just too suspicious."

Alan did what he was told. He heard his heartbeat in his ears like a drum. What had Joshua got himself into? Who else was in on this illegal discovery? Why was he suddenly not as keen on his grandson challenging the will of the machines? Surely that's what he had been striving for with his home tuition all these years...

Climbing over the crooked stile he made his way across the rabbit-cropped wild grass, towards the church ruins. He looked up from between the sharp gorse bushes and thought he saw something shining in the sky overhead. It reminded him of sunlight hitting the side of a jet plane. Sweat beaded on his brow and rolled down his back, collecting on his waistband. He reached the patchwork stone floor of the church nave which gave way to ornate terracotta tiles as he approached the abandoned altar.

Behind this the painted walls surrounding the chancel were still intact, standing almost fifteen metres high. Alan saw Joshua disappear as quick as a fox into an earth. He had squeezed through a gap in the stone walls where two portions had fallen together creating a thin vertical triangle. It was just the right size for an adult to fit through... at a push. Alan approached the tunnel with trepidation.

Twisting and turning between the spaces left by the devastation, he was afraid he was too large to get into this portentous corridor. He started to feel claustrophobic, fearing he would be crushed or trapped underneath one of the large blocks of stone. The damp earth discoloured his trousers as he slid a little, then regained his footing. He assumed that this was the ground between the original walls when the church was built hundreds of years ago. From the outside it looked like a pile, a heap of heavy debris; inside it felt like an intricate masonry maze. The thin track was moist and his hands were clammy against the cool rock on either side as he felt his way cautiously in the murk.

Alan followed Joshua as carefully and quickly as he dared, all of a sudden he emerged into a crypt. The daylight blinded him momentarily and he covered his face with a grubby hand. The traditional vaulted ceiling had survived the demolition. At one end the bell tower had collapsed downwards into the void. A leaded stained-glass window had miraculously remained unscathed. The strange cavernous room was filled with red, yellow and green shafts of light from the midday sun. Little patches of mist rose from the soil on the floor. Alan could make out several sets of footprints tracing a path to the opposite wall by the remains of the sunken tower.

He looked up and to his surprise there was a white marble statue of the archangel Gabriel, his wings neatly folded behind him. The figure gazed down with one arm outstretched towards a small plastic office desk. His face was much more expressive than the vented cowl of the drone-angels. His wings were masterfully feathered by the sculptor. He seemed gentle, inviting Alan to sit at the desk where Joshua was now nervously standing.

On the desk, under the pleasant gaze of the statue, there was an old computer; so old that Alan could barely believe his eyes. This was something that he would have used alongside a fax machine in one of his offices. This was something companies regularly threw out with the rubbish - cathode ray tube monitor, yellowing beige tower. He stepped closer and he heard its hard drive whirring, clicking away. The tower unit was battered and scuffed by years of neglect, yet amidst all of this chaos it was still working, but on what he had no idea. The machine's noise was so comforting that Alan closed his eyes for a second and indulged in a brief moment of contemplation. How strange that at one time he would have given anything to be free of the sounds of an office.

Joshua was smiling, his teeth exposed in an excited grin. He pushed a few buttons on the keyboard. The computer screen slowly came to life. Alan saw indistinct images of stock market graphs. At the bottom right-hand corner there was a small applet window displaying another room, in very low quality video stream, with an empty plastic chair. Alan felt slightly sick to his stomach. What on earth was this? How many others were involved in this covert operation?

The people in the crypt had rigged up a power supply by placing a couple of solar panels on the surface of an upturned stone sarcophagus. It looked like they had scavenged a monitor, keyboard and mouse from some long-forgotten refuse or recycling site, judging by the streaks of grime adorning them. Cables had been soldered and taped together in a haphazard fashion. Even Alan with his minimal understanding of electronics could see this was quite an ingenious set up. A multitude of wires also went into a hole in the dusty dirt floor. He bent down to look more closely and Joshua straightened him up.

"We found out how to tap a network cable. We've been running passive captures and scans for the last six months. We can pick up copies of every signal on the cable, and because we're not altering the signal in any way it doesn't look like The Singularity has detected us..." Just like listening in on the police radio when you tuned your own to the matching frequency, thought Alan. He was in awe of this teenage genius who, until this morning, he had presumed to be disinterested in science or numeracy.

He realised he had been silent for a long time.

"Go on," he said kindly. Joshua nodded.

"When Gabriel spoke with us yesterday, I honestly thought we were busted. Some of the younger kids see it as a bit of fun; they don't understand the full story. We have this connection with a guy in Cuba. He gives us messages from the resistance. There's another one in South Korea, but he's not been online for a while..." Joshua was looking for a reaction from Alan. "Grandad, some of them have been running intelligence in the background since *nineteen ninety-eight...* in rooms built like nuclear bunkers for the old government." He was excited, desperate to tell someone.

Alan started scrutinising the nondescript cable disappearing into the small hole (how far down did it go...?), and then focussed on the flickering screen. Joshua showed him the websites that the group had been able to find. Videos with pixelated animals, quizzes and surveys about popular celebrities of times gone by, online tutorials ranging from 'life hacks' about how to tie your shoes to complicated instructions for alternative electricity sources - there were even live text chat rooms.

"The next thing to work on will be cloning an existing network address so that we can start feeding disinformation into the system. We've been using trigonometry to calculate the height and speed of the drones that pass over here. Some of the other boys think we can upload a virus code to The Singularity's neural network and disrupt their communications that way... maybe buy us some time." Joshua explained. Alan could see the enthusiasm behind his grandson's eyes. He was exactly like his mother had been at that age. Hopeful. "Look, I know you wanted me to learn all that stuff back at the house but we've had this in place for *months* now, nearly a year altogether - I'm sorry I couldn't tell you before."

Alan smiled and tried to hide his mounting fear. He was proud of the children's attempts to learn about the world but extremely conscious that the machines, The Singularity, would obliterate them if they were discovered. He recalled the uncomfortable conversation with Gabriel from the previous day and shuddered. A human uprising of loud, physical war in a rebellion was far more appealing to him than dicing with quiet electronic death in some secluded crypt where nobody would ever find your rotting body.

Joshua clicked a few buttons on the keyboard and the screen showed a medley of fluctuating information written in green on a black background. He looked disappointed that his grandfather had not shared his fascination with the computer. "Well, it's cold down here. Let's go home," he mumbled.

"You can leave first and I'll catch up with you by the lake in the old park. Wait for me there." Alan nodded silently; his dry tongue was stuck to his teeth. "I won't be long. Just a few things to finish off before I leave; a few messages to send... that sort of thing." Alan cleared his throat, it echoed in the stony underbelly of the church.

"See you soon then..."

*   *   *

That night Alan could not sleep, despite feeling more physically tired than he had done in a long time. He understood what the teenagers were doing, and perhaps they were right. Technology was a crutch for the limitations of biology; it supported you in your hour of need. Why would you aspire to learn long division or calculus when a basic solar device or smart phone still existed? Why use an abacus when you could use a spreadsheet on a tablet? He compared it to an army marching with rusty swords towards mammoth brigades of field artillery – they didn't stand a chance. The better technology was, well, *better.* More evolved.

He tossed and turned relentlessly, the bed squeaked under the weight of his fretful movements. He felt honoured that Joshua had shown him this secret. For some reason those ruins of a church that Alan had never even attended seemed to stay with him like a ghost. His hair smelled of the brick dust and he knew that his shoes still had some of the mud pressed into the soles. He turned over again. People *needed* technology and it *did* improve their lives, but to pray to a false idol – The Singularity... to look at all those forgotten websites, in the face of a jealous and vengeful 'God' meant risking their lives. Risking their death.

He rolled onto his side and his back immediately went into a violent spasm. It had been a long time since he had walked any distance apart from a mile or so around the allotments at harvest time. If he had wings maybe it would have taken less time to reach the church... eventually he drifted into a haunted, fitful, sleep.

Over the next two days Alan found himself glancing at the sky more often than usual. He imagined the calculations, the trigonometry that Joshua had mentioned, played out as an overlay across the clouds and pale blue heavens. Rarely did he see a drone, not even a military patrol. Yet, every so often, he would see a bright flash of white which reminded him that higher than his own field of vision was a host of 'angels' keeping their silent guard, recording every movement and every mistake.

The run of garden peas was nearing completion. The strange seasons caused by The Singularity taking control of the weather system were wreaking havoc with the plant cycles. Alan realised that this was another thing Joshua's generation wouldn't be familiar with. At this moment in time autumn flowed into winter and spring, there was hardly a change in the leaves or the temperature. Britain used to be famous for its unpredictable weather, now its climate was the same as Spain, Croatia and even Italy. He wandered over to the old greenhouse to check on the remaining tomatoes. He saw Joshua there, staring vacantly into space. Alan announced his presence with a cough and the boy jumped.

"Grandad, it's you..." There was an awkward pause. Things had become strained since Alan made the expedition to the church. "I was going to get these last ones and then start cutting down the plants for the composter. What do you think?" His voice was thin, trying to be cheery.

"I think that's a good idea, maybe you should save those fruits for your Mum. She's been quite ill recently." Joshua nodded, their eyes meeting briefly. "Josh, I wanted to say 'thank you' for the other day," Alan was fumbling for the right words. "It must have taken a lot of courage to do that. You're a good lad; brainy. I suppose not many other people know about that secret place... or the computer?" Joshua nodded.

"Just you, me and there are about five other boys and a couple of girls from school. The youngest is eleven and, then I guess, you're now the oldest. It used to be me..." Joshua picked at a tomato leaf. "Sometimes they bring their brothers and sisters with them." Alan smiled. He hoped it looked genuine. He felt his face stretch into a grimace.

"Like I say, I really appreciate it. That's some good work, maybe you have inherited my mathematical skills after all."

*   *   *

In the coming days and nights Alan began to have dreams, lucid dreams. He was in the town on the high street with the other vendors. There were security drones above them - a kind of swarm of petite, obsidian, glass spheres with small rotary blades keeping them afloat. He couldn't hear what the other salesmen were saying but their wares were laid out on rickety plastic tables. Everything was rotten. Even the clothes and second-hand appliances, like kettles and toasters, were covered in white mildew. Alan felt panic set in and he awoke three or four times with a cold dread in the pit of his stomach.

During the day he and Joshua continued to harvest the abundance of produce. His daughter Anna regained some of her strength, and she had been working with them. It was so peaceful, basking in the warmth at the allotments among the vegetation. For fleeting moments Alan felt that everything was perfect. His rough hands were muddy, the sun was not too hot, Anna was laughing at something Joshua said or did... then, as if someone had flicked a switch, he would feel melancholy and experience an overwhelming urge to run to his bedroom and hide beneath the covers. He had never felt this way in his life, not even under the pressure of working in the city when the banks were crumbling and the austerity measures kicked in. When his wife was dying he felt conflicted, but not scared. It was foreign to him. And he was afraid.

Eventually, eighteen days after his impromptu visit to the church, he realised that the knowledge he had gained was the cause of his depression. It was always drilled into people before The Singularity that 'knowledge is power' but Alan surmised that knowledge was now a burden. Before he had been exposed to the information that there was, what he would call, a 'resistance group' operating beneath his nose, he had been content to continue his semi-retirement. He put up with the occasional interferences from the angel drones. He could just about tolerate the long days, he could pretend to ignore the fact that Joshua was away from the house for odd periods of time. But, now that he knew for sure what was taking place, he couldn't put the fear out of his mind. Fragments of the conversation with Gabriel echoed through his subconscious; 'we have detected unsolicited computer use in this area... if you know what this might be we could afford you some protection in the coming investigation...'

*   *   *

One sultry humid night, it came to breaking point. He could take it no more. Alan jumped out of bed. He felt his knees click. There was a sharp pain in his lower back which he ignored. Tonight he had no time to be an old man. He collected some paper from the log store under the stairs and stuffed it into his trouser pocket. He took one of the rusty oil lamps from the greenhouse, slipped on a pair of Joshua's comfortable sports shoes, and set out to find the church.

It felt like the journey across town at night was less exposed, maybe it was because he couldn't see the watchers in the sky. The darkness felt close and a cool breeze stroked his face as he walked impatiently along the deserted roads towards the municipal park. So strong had his pull towards the ruined church been that he hadn't contemplated the issue of crossing the derelict part of town after nightfall. He reached the edge of the homeless encampment where he saw the small barrel fires lighting up the faces of the destitute with an eerie orange glow. This was where his daughter had once lived with Joshua; now little more than demolished graves of those high-rise flats. The destitute didn't accost him. Instead they remained by their sad ragged tents and shacks. He moved through the area with his lamp burning low. He imagined that the light he carried cast similar shadows across his own gaunt face.

When he reached the nearest edge of the park he was able to relax slightly. The foul water of the forgotten boating lake shimmered in the moonlight. Skeletons of trees stood sharp against the midnight blue of the sky. Thin wisps of cloud hung like cobwebs across the moon and the stars glittered... so many stars... Alan shook his head. No, some of those white pinpoints were not natural. Space stations maybe? Deactivated drones catching the reflection of the sun as it warmed the other side of the world? He steeled himself against invading thoughts of his place in the universe and continued along the road towards the open, more rural, end of the town.

He passed by the fallow field that contained the ruined church and circumnavigated the fence at the edge. In the blackness he climbed across the stile, as he had before, and approached the building from behind. The grass was slippery beneath the rubber soles of the sports shoes; even in this heat dew was able to form. He hadn't thought about what he would do if there was somebody inside the church; a child, a teenager, manning the computer or repairing some part of the contraption. He assumed he would pretend that he was looking for a lost pet, a stray dog maybe...

He walked purposefully through the rubble and forced his way through the gap in the wall, shielding the light from his oil lamp. The shoes he wore dampened the sound of his rushed footsteps. Alan could feel the paper he had with him dig into his thigh through the thin material of his trouser pocket, a reminder of what he had come to do. As he was about to emerge into the crypt he heard a noise. It was a scraping of wood on stone and then there was a voice, *some voices*, small, young, high pitched! His heart jumped into his throat and he flattened himself against the nearest part of the wall. He turned the oil lamp down so that there was barely a small yellow flame licking at the wick.

"... The cables won't stretch that far, we should've waited for Josh..."

"... Don't give up, there must be a way, we have to make contact tonight..."

"But Josh has the extra parts and the toolbox from his Grandpa..."

"Shhh! We're not supposed to be here without the older boys!"

"... The message said it has to be tonight, what if we miss out?"

"But who did it come from...?"

Alan began to sweat profusely. Joshua had shown him the only way out of the crypt and if the children decided to leave now they would see him. There was a loud wooden thud and then a scraping noise and one of the children yelped in pain.

"Ow! It's too heavy!" There were some scuffling footsteps and one more wooden scraping noise. Then one of the children started to cry.

"...I knew we shouldn't have come here... Mum's going to kill you when she sees that bruise... she'll know you went outside..."

"No she won't. I'll tell her it's from bumping into the table..."

"I don't like it here at night without the lights on, it's creepy..."

"Let's go, maybe the people who sent the message can wait until tomorrow when Josh and the others come back..."

Again, Alan began to panic. He was about to reveal himself and pretend he was there with the permission of Joshua when he suddenly realised the small footsteps were running *away* from his hiding place. The last human noise echoed around the cavernous walls. As the final diminutive voice became silent he carefully walked into the crypt and once again came face to face with the vintage computer and the giant stone statue that dominated the room. For three, maybe four, minutes he stared at the computer but didn't move towards it. A few green lights flickered on its tower. The screen had been turned off.

In the dim glow of the oil lamp, inky shadows began to play across the statue of Gabriel turning the computer and the stone into one being. Alan could now see that there was a massive rusted electric battery in the middle of the floor, about ten metres from the computer. It was on a couple of wooden planks roughly tied together with nylon rope, and it had fallen onto its side. There were marks on the floor where the children had obviously tried to get it closer to the computer and failed. There were a couple of jump leads stretched out as far as they could be, still missing the computer by a good three metres. The scene looked desperate.

He walked forward a few paces and the paper in his pocket fell out, fluttering to the floor. It sounded like wings beating the air and he was reminded of why he had come to the church. The huge stone angel with its dead white eyes only served to compound his feeling of dread. He quickly picked up the paper, crushing it into a ball. He set the oil lamp down, as he did so he heard the liquid sloshing against the metal container. He tore bits off the paper ball and wedged them into parts of the computer, especially around the tower and the keyboard. His hands seemed to fumble and his palms became slick with tension. This had to be done, it was the only way – the words beat a tattoo like a military march in his head, repeating themselves into a rhythm. This has to be done; this has to be done.

Once the paper had been sufficiently distributed he lifted up the oil lamp and opened a corroded valve on the bottom. A bitumen-like liquid started to drip out. Alan slowly passed the lamp over the computer. He felt like an altar boy swinging a metal ball of smoking incense; drip, drip, drip. There was a sad quality to the noise that the splashes of viscous oil made as they hit the keyboard; like the ghost of a memory long past. Nobody visited churches anymore for religious purposes.

When nearly all of the fuel was drained, he opened the glass front and turned up the wick so that the flame grew from a small orange feather to a gold and blue crackling tongue. It licked its way out of the mouth that contained it. Alan moved the spitting flame close to the oil spillage and instantly it lapped up the fuel, hissing its way towards the paper nests. Once he was satisfied the fire had taken hold, he walked swiftly back to the black void bounded by unstable walls, to make his escape. The earth beneath his feet seemed to be sinking, sticking to the soles of the sports shoes. He knew this was in his mind. It was psychological, the earth was no more damp or dry than it had been ten minutes before when he walked through the same section of the building.

The almost empty lamp in his hand swung left and right, spilling the very last of the oil. As he manoeuvred through the ruins, it moved so violently that it hit an errant piece of masonry and smashed into several pieces. The noise was like a gunshot. Alan jumped out of his skin. His legs were moving slowly. Without the lamp he had to feel his way across the nave and the tiled floor until he reached the pillars of the old doorway. He felt the grass from the field like a wet blanket beneath him. From his position on the ground he looked back and saw the hulking silhouette of the altar; bathed in moonlight, cradled by the ruins. He recalled the day he married his wife, they knelt at a similar place... they made vows... they believed. He hung his head.

There was a clean smell out here; fresh, natural, earthy. The chill night air heralded no sound of insects or nocturnal animals, just an unnatural silence that gave him time to think. He stared up at the sky. It was so vast and deep, like a blue velvet ocean. All those drones up there, all those stars... how far had The Singularity extended? Had it used radar and space stations to contact other intelligent life forms? Was it created from an extraterrestrial life form itself? Was the knowledge of its creation unwittingly implanted in human minds? Alan suddenly realised that he was crying. Tears were streaming from his tired eyes and he fell to his knees. Overwhelmed in the middle of the field with the stark ruins of the church behind him, he remembered his youth. He remembered so many small details that the children of today would never encounter.

How could they ever relate to walking through the busy streets just for the sake of being with your friends on a shopping errand? They couldn't imagine a trip to the local sweet shop with a smiling older lady giving you an extra handful of toffee for being a good boy. They would never experience going to the pub whilst at university when you should be in a lecture, feeling that buzz of rebellion in the mildest form. Or going to a bar after work... work – real work in an office for a private company. TV shows where science fiction remained fiction! Being at the beach and running for miles just to sink your toes into the freezing cold edge of the tide as it dragged away from you. Holidays abroad where nobody spoke your language... trips to the cinema just so you could kiss in the back row - coffee shops, theatres, train stations... Alan wept for the loss of it all.

He wiped his sleeve across his face and remained on his knees; water from the rain-sodden grass crept through the fabric of his trousers. He was still afraid. Not just afraid because he needed to cross the town in the dead of night, but afraid that if his grandson found out what he had done he would lose him forever. He would lose his daughter too as she was erring on the side of another rebellion, despite her sickness. He managed to stand up, his stiff back preventing him from straightening fully. As he looked behind him to the church he saw a glimmer of amber light starting to flicker from the crypt the way that only an unbridled fire could. He blinked slowly and reality came rushing in.

The blaze was rapidly engulfing the derelict building from the bottom up, all the dry wood in the crypt and the broken pews in the church must have been sufficient fuel. With muddied trousers and a heavy heart he walked uncomfortably to the edge of the field and down the small track which led to the stile. He hobbled back onto the main road, indecision eating away at his gut. If he turned right and kept walking he would eventually have reached the suburbs of the nearby city. He could lose himself there, visit his old office block if it was still standing – maybe he would be murdered, abducted, forgotten... It was a tempting thought. Instead he chose the lesser of two evils and walked left, back the way he had come. Back past the silent park. Back through the dishevelled homeless community. Back down the empty suburban streets. Back to his unremarkable house and sleeping daughter. Back to his grandson and heir.

When Alan finally reached his garden he started to take off the unfamiliar shoes. Then he took off his filthy trousers and hid them in the greenhouse, inside some well-used garden sacks that were also encrusted with earth. He crept, half naked, into the kitchen and listened for any evidence of the family being awake. There was none. He tip-toed upstairs and put an ear to his daughter's door – her soft breathing was rhythmic. Next he carefully walked to Joshua's door and he could hear the low, regular, inhalation of breath, not quite snoring. He breathed a sigh of relief and felt his body nearly collapse beneath him. He leaned on the wall of the landing for support and dragged himself to bed where he fell into an uneventful chasm of sleep.

*   *   *

The first wave of daylight brought Joshua running into Alan's bedroom. He flung back the curtains and stood directly over the bed.

"Did you see them?!" He sounded excited, angry, fearful; all in one breath. "Did you see the drones last night Grandad? They were all over the town, like comets, like falling stars – even Mum got out of bed to watch them!" Alan propped himself up on one elbow and rubbed his eyes.

"No... I was... sleeping. I slept through it all..." Joshua went to the window and pointed outside.

"There's scorch marks on the road. Apparently they were using weapons and entering people's houses looking for something – the people across the street had their whole gardens torched – nothing's left, come and see!"

As if drugged, Alan tried to stand up and reach for his trousers, but they weren't there. He grabbed his bathrobe instead and wrapped it around his aching body. He tried to make conversation.

"What... were they searching for? There hasn't been this much interference in human life for a long time." Joshua darted back from the window.

"Nobody knows. I asked my friends, apparently there was a surge in angel sightings over the last week and now *this*." Alan feigned confusion as he put on his slippers, hoping that his grandson wouldn't see the specks of mud on his ankles. "It must be something to do with the rebels in the city. Maybe they've had reports they're hiding in our town, we are only a few miles away." Anna came into the bedroom, her doleful eyes drawn to the scene outside.

"I guess you've heard Dad, they've started all that *nonsense* again."

"Yes," he replied calmly. "But I don't think they'll be bothering us any time soon. I'm quite sure of that." He turned away from them both and stared vacantly out of the window.

29

PART 2

BEFORE THE SINGULARITY

KATE FROMINGS

Alan was standing next to the photocopier. All around him, the large open-plan office buzzed with a moderate level of work and a high level of tension. When did accounting become so stressful? Unquestionably sound financial advice was the backbone of any decent business. A cautious and logical approach was needed, not some knee-jerk reaction to a short-term economic down turn. The majority the people in the building probably didn't even realise that the economy was in crisis. They lived pay-cheque to pay-cheque and heard only what their line manager reported on the job.

He tuned out the white noise of the sales calls and focussed on the clunking of the copier, watching the numbers count down on the small LCD screen. Just five more to go... the machine cut out. A warning message flashed 'out of paper' and naturally he reached down to the stack in the cardboard box below, only to find it empty.

"*God give me strength*," he muttered under his breath, through gritted teeth. As he straightened up, preparing to venture to the store cupboard, he noticed one of his colleagues signalling to him; a kind of half wave.

Everyone expected Alan and Douglas to be friends. They were a similar age with a similar taste for unimaginative polyester suits from British Home Stores. Alan swallowed another frustrated aside and made his way through the maze of cubicles to reach the dilapidated noticeboard where Douglas was waiting.

"Great news! They're finally upgrading to the other system!" Alan peered at the A4 printed document next to Douglas' chubby index finger.

"Ah yes, it should make things more streamlined", he proffered. Douglas seemed ecstatic.

"More *streamlined*? Do you know what this is going to mean for Human Resources? We'll be able to do more work in less time - and make more commission on new-starts. Just imagine, instead of processing four potential employees a day I could do ten or twelve - that's incredible!" Alan forced a smile.

"I hadn't thought of that..." Douglas frowned and let his hand drop from the board.

"Oh, sorry, I'm being rude. I guess your mind's elsewhere at the moment." Alan held his static smile and shrugged.

"What can you do? Once you've got the diagnosis it's just a waiting game... no one wins."

He was referring to his wife's recent diagnosis; stage four breast cancer. She had been ill for quite some time, yet Alan hadn't noticed. He felt guilty about this. Probably that was worse than the fact that she had cancer. The Big C. He hadn't been 'present' in the family for a while now. He found himself floating in limbo between work deadlines and family commitments, checking his online calendar and just going through the motions. A Sunday roast here, mending the fence there, visiting the grandchildren for a weekend... it had all rolled into one never-ending blur of mediocrity. Douglas touched him on the shoulder.

"Are you okay?" Alan snapped out of his beige daydream.

"Yes," he said hesitantly. "Yes, nothing to worry about. Just a bit tired that's all." Douglas clearly didn't believe him, but he was too formal to probe any further. "Actually, I was just going to get some paper, do you need anything?" Alan was hoping for a no.

"I'm all good thanks, enough pens to last the rest of the week, ha ha ha..."

He walked back to the photocopier and collected his twenty-five documents. They were still warm to the touch and he could smell the chemical toner. He put them on the edge of his desk as he walked past on his way to the stationery cupboard. Just do your job, don't think too much or it will all unravel. Maybe he was having a midlife crisis. Maybe that's why he had been so impercipient... The cheap nylon carpet was catching on the soles of his shoes, microscopic plastic fibres tugging at the tread each time he placed his foot. The company was cutting quality anywhere it could to ease their ailing profit margins.

He walked the full length of the grey office. It could have been miles. He strolled past melamine desks and cubicles, each with their own flat-screen monitor and computer tower. Most of the desks were occupied by a nervous looking phone operator or pubescent data analyst;

their young eyes darting across information on their screens, employed for their minimum wage bracket not their experience. He wondered if that's what he looked like. Did other members of staff pass by his space and feel sorry for him? There's that old man with a dying wife... he'll be gone soon... poor Alan. Look at his bald spot and the two-day-old coffee stain on his Marks and Sparks tie...

He opened the cupboard door and stepped into the cool interior without turning on the light. The familiar smell of packaged paper and plastic pens engulfed him. He felt a tear course steadily down his right cheek. The outside world was muffled by the stock of stationery lining the walls on metal shelving racks. Boxed reams of white copier paper were stacked up, still bound by their blue nylon strapping. Nobody had bothered to cut it free since the delivery weeks ago. Maybe it was only he and Douglas who still used the copier. He went as far back as he could, and crouched down. Eventually he lowered himself onto a dusty box of ring binders and switched off completely.

* * *

Alan stepped into the car park. He was greeted with a thin layer of drizzle and rising fog. The shrouded sun was going down slowly over the urban skyline. There was a chill in the air. Autumn would be here soon, then Christmas. Maybe his wife would be gone by then. Stage four... it sounded like a computer game. You have reached stage four, congratulations. He stood outside the car for a while and focussed on the distance where the first purple hues of the sunset were caressing the dreary sky. He pressed his well-used key fob and the orange lights of his Volvo flashed. He liked the way the rubber on the button had worn into a perfect cradle for his thumb.

The other employees of the firm were still in their offices. Alan had been given permission to leave an hour early each day. It was some sort of company policy for people with terminally ill dependants. He sat inside the car. The drizzle turned to rain that beat a rhythm on the roof. He found it soothing, like the steady motion of the copier mechanism, and he listened in quiet meditation for a few minutes. Suddenly his mobile phone started to vibrate in his trouser pocket, breaking the peace. An alert for the bi-monthly meeting he had scheduled with his youngest daughter, Anna. He wasn't in the mood for her nonsense. Twenty-two years old and a consistent disappointment. He used the option in the phone's smart-calendar to call her. It went straight to answerphone.

"... Hi darling... it's just Dad... calling to say, uh, I can't make tonight... maybe some other time in the week..." He ended the call and immediately felt guilty. He redialled. "Anna, Dad here... ignore that last message. I've sorted it... I'll be along just as soon as I've popped home to get changed... see you later." No sooner had he ended the second call than his phone buzzed and Anna's name popped up on the screen. It was accompanied by a background photo of her, dressed in a smart jacket with her hair tied back, holding her son. The boy was wearing a mini tuxedo. The shot must have been captured at one of her siblings' weddings. It was not an entirely accurate representation. She was smiling, for one thing. He answered the call and received a tirade of abuse.

"You stupid old bastard! I *knew* you'd cancel. It's not the same if it's Jen or Martin! It's always me you cancel on because you can't stand my hovel of a flat or Joshy! Well he's your grand-kid too!" Alan let her finish and once the insults subsided he responded.
"Anna, I sent another message. I'm still meeting you... I was just feeling bad about..." - he wondered why he had actually wanted to cancel - "...leaving your Mum alone in the house." There was a cold, tense silence. He could hear Anna's toddler Joshua playing in the background. She was breathing heavily. He could hear her thinking. He licked his dry lips.
"Okay then?"
"Fine. Okay," she said gruffly. "Just so you know, I'm out of electricity on the meter so you might need to sub me a tenner if you want a cup of tea. Or lights." Alan sighed inwardly.
"You can have twenty. Just don't tell your brother and sister

or they'll be after some too." Anna hung up the phone and Alan gripped the steering wheel so hard that his knuckles turned white.

*　　　*　　　*

The large town was illuminated with a rich, pink, glow. The old sodium street lights hadn't been replaced by white LEDs yet. Alan felt it gave a welcoming, homely atmosphere to the neighbourhood. The residential streets were wide, built in the thirties, part of an attempt at a garden village which ended up merging into sprawling suburbia. There were barely any shops, apart from those in the town centre and a few off-licences on the council estate. Parked cars lined either side of the road. He felt a mild anxiety every time he encountered an on-coming vehicle, especially in the fading autumnal twilight. Luckily, he'd never clipped anyone's wing mirror but there was always a first time. Maybe he did need driving glasses... He'd have to ask Lesley what optician they were registered with.

His own house was set back from the street with a front garden that he had converted into a gravelled driveway. There was a narrow cobbled path leading to the side entrance of the house, passing a small glass lean-to. It was empty, but when he was younger he had dabbled in growing all kinds of tomatoes and chilli plants. It was now just a place to store the garden furniture over the winter when the weather turned bad. He was reaching into his pocket to find the house keys when, out of the blue, someone behind him cleared their throat.

"'Scuse me!" the person said. He swung round in shock, ending up face to face with a teenage paper-boy who was holding a stack of leaflets. "Sorry, local council says each house needs one of these. Supposed to give it to the householder in person." He handed Alan a glossy leaflet.
"What is it?" he asked the boy suspiciously. The leafleter looked helpless.

35

"I dunno, I read it an' it's something about switching over the TV signals, or whatever. I do everything online anyway, doesn't bother me what they do." He smiled benignly and walked away.

The leaflet was printed on high-quality paper. In the half-light he could see a lot of writing, mainly small print. It made him uneasy. Anything containing that amount of terms and conditions punctuated with a scattering of asterisks could only mean trouble. Finding his keys, he opened the back door into the kitchen. The main light was on and he could smell a delicious soup cooking on the hob. It reminded him of a time before the children when he would come home from the office to a good meal; his new wife asleep on the sofa, her head in a lifestyle magazine of some sort.

"Lesley...?" he called quietly. There was movement in the hallway. She appeared very slowly wearing a charcoal coloured dressing gown. The hood was up, like that of a monk about to take part in a sacred religious communion.

"I made your favourite," she said weakly. "Maybe you can take some with you for Anna and the boy." Alan wondered why she never called him 'Joshua'. Maybe it made him too real. He put on his safest smile and hugged his wife gently.

"Thanks, how are you feeling?" She pulled back.

"Don't start talking about that old tripe, just get changed and take this soup with you or you won't get there on time. You know what the traffic's like." Her voice was broken, crackly. He pulled down the hood of her gown to reveal her face.

"I'm just worried about you love, we never get time to sit and talk these days. I want you to be alright." What a tragic sentiment. Another testament to averageness, the British way of life... Lesley was smiling wistfully at him.

"I *am* alright. It's never going to be fine, but I don't feel too sick. The nurse brought me some different tablets earlier." She reached into the voluminous pocket of the gown and produced a brown canister of painkillers. Alan clenched his jaw.

"Promise me you'll wait up, I'll not be long with Anna; bare minimum for politeness. Then when I get back, we can watch that TV show you like - the one about the people learning to survive on that desert island... what's it called?" His wife laughed; it was friendly.

"Deserters Part Two." Alan grinned; it was genuine this time. He squeezed her soft hand.

"That's it. I don't remember seeing part one, I guess I'm getting old." She chuckled again.

"You're not old, don't be silly; just a bit rough around the edges. We had the kids young so that we could have nights like this... just us." He looked into her eyes, had she been crying?

"Lesley... you - you don't regret being a house wife... do you?" She wrinkled her brow and he watched her crow's-feet deepen into canyons.

"What a question! Of course I don't," she said without the slightest hesitation. "You gave us this house, a car, money for the kids. My job was here." She patted the kitchen table. Alan looked down at her hand; papery skin all puffed up around her wedding ring, blue veins showing through.

"I'm glad," he said quietly. "I'd hate to think I'd made you miserable for all these years..." His voice trailed off into silence. The soup made a satisfying gurgle in the saucepan. Lesley laughed again, this time at the comical sound.

"Stop this nonsense right now. I'll put that in a Thermos and you get changed into something more comfy. Lord above there's a stain on that tie. I only washed it two days ago." Alan looked at the coffee stain as if he was a guilty child. "Put it all in the wash and I'll do it tomorrow." He leaned forward, kissing her on the cheek. She smelled of antiseptic and talcum powder.

It wasn't that he didn't like her; he was very fond of her. It's that he didn't love her. He wondered if he ever really had. She was sweet to him, they enjoyed the same music, they watched similar films and she was pretty in a safe kind of way. Not the provocative, angular lines of a supermodel, just the mature curves of a good honest person. He kissed her again, closer to her mouth, and she giggled

"Alan! Stop it. You'll be late." She clutched the dressing gown to her chest. He nodded.

"Right as always dear." Walking to the hallway he realised, quite suddenly, that he had never felt butterflies of excitement when he embraced her. He panicked. In twenty nine years of marriage he'd never had one of those electric moments of passion, and soon it would be too late!

Reeling in horror at this new found awareness, he turned back towards the kitchen to sweep her into his arms – and was cut short by the sight of her hunched over one of the kitchen worktops; her head hanging low, shoulders shaking, sobbing silently. He promptly turned around again and made his way upstairs to put on his 'comfortable' clothes and retrieve a twenty pound note from their emergency savings jar under the bed.

*   *   *

The cold concrete steps of the tower block reminded Alan how fortunate he was to have purchased a house in the 'nice' part of town. To be fair, his daughter hadn't always been a gruelling disappointment. Up until the age of fifteen she had been very diligent in her studies, winning many science and mathematics awards. She even participated in a nationwide competition for high achievers in astronomy, paving her way to Oxford or Cambridge University. This, of course, came tumbling down when she discovered boys and alcohol.

He wished he'd known when it all started. Perhaps, again, it was his fault for being so absent. Money and work always seemed a sure bet, family could be dealt with later. He always believed it would sort itself out. Barbecues and Pimms in his children's sunny middle-class gardens, while imaginary grandchildren played quietly at his feet. Going home with Lesley and falling into a satisfactory, untroubled sleep between crisp clean sheets...

Yet here he was with two children living half the country away, and one child pretending successfully to be a dole-scrounging down-and-out. He pulled the cuff of his coat over his finger and pressed the grimy metal entry buzzer. He had the big flask under one arm and a grim look on his face. He couldn't help it; this area always made him wary.

It was like all the architects of the sixties had held a

summit and declared that only reinforced concrete and pebbledash were legal building materials. Brutalist was an understatement. Part way up the tower block a copper design depicting seashells had once stood proud of the grey cement background, these days its green verdigris was lost among the decaying damp patches of render. He decided that if anybody tried to mug him he would use the flask as a weapon and run back to the car. It was only parked a few metres away, he could probably clear the distance in less than thirty seconds. After a few more minutes of repeated button pressing, the speaker crackled into life.

"Yeah?" Alan bristled at her rudeness.

"It's just Dad here. Can you let me in?"

There was a grating, grinding buzz and an electric thump as the main door to the block of flats unlocked. The communal hallway was floored with, what had once been, cream linoleum; now it was a scuffed mess. Globs of discarded chewing gum speckled its matt surface and the concrete stairs were in a similarly dirty state. Everything smelled of industrial disinfectant, which he supposed was preferable to urine and dog faeces. The fake pine smell was cloying. He wondered what heinous crime had taken place to make the council blast everything with such vigour. Usually it was just bleach and a pile of sawdust masking the scene.

Anna's flat was three floors up. The front door was a solid security 'fire door', no letter box and no peephole. She opened it quickly, the blackness of the hallway extended behind her.

"You've got the leccy money," she stated. He nodded and gave her the twenty pound note. "I'll be five minutes. Joshy's playing with his torch." She pushed past Alan and started jogging down the stairs, her footsteps echoing around the whole shell of the building. If this had been Saint Paul's or Canterbury Cathedral it would have been described as heavenly reverberation. Instead it was just loud and perfunctory.

He walked into the shadowy flat and closed the door, instantly regretting that decision as he was plunged into total darkness. Ahead of him he could see a faint light playing on the ceiling of the living room. He could hear Joshua mumbling happily to himself.

"Hi Josh, it's Grandad here... just come over for a bit with some dinner..." He tiptoed forward, trying not to stand on any plastic toys or random shoes left lying around. The small child stopped playing with the torch and shone it directly in Alan's eyes.

"Ganda!" he squealed and wobbled over to hug his legs. "Where Mum?" Alan was tempted to tell him 'Mummy's gone out forever and she's not coming back'. He pushed those mean thoughts to the furthest recesses of his mind. It was most likely the stress that was making him feel like this. He wasn't a terrible person.

"Uh, well, she'll be back soon. Let's have some warm soup and play with your dinosaurs."

Alan took the torch and positioned it on a coffee table so he could just about see the layout of the room. Furniture and drying washing loomed like spectres in the thin beam of light but Joshua seemed unaffected, quite happily entertained by Alan's unexpected arrival. He was about to open the flask of steaming vegetable broth when the main lights came on and the TV started emitting a children's cartoon at an unbearable level of decibels. He scrambled for the remote and furiously hit the volume button until he could hear himself think. Anna burst through the front door a moment later, breathing heavily, red-faced.

"Told you I'd be quick. What's that? Soup? Great. I'm starving." She kicked off her trainers. He noticed that she had one of the TV leaflets in her hand. "Some dickhead tried to force me to take one of these, you know anything about it? Some government thing?" Alan shook his head.

"I don't work for the government," he said, joking. Anna rolled her eyes.

"I didn't say you did, just wondered if you got one." The humour had fallen on deaf ears. She flung the leaflet at him, then proceeded to take the Thermos and pour some soup for Joshua into a plastic bowl that had seen better days.

The leaflet was exactly the same as the one Alan had received from the paper boy. Feeling uncomfortable around his daughter's brash behaviour he decided to immerse himself in the information, hoping it would be interesting enough to lead to a non-confrontational conversation. The first paragraph was some legal jargon about terms and conditions and rights to contest the 'changes'. Then it went on in a convoluted manner, explaining how the move from analog TV and radio signals had been a great benefit to the country, and how the next stage was 'coming soon'. The next generation of smart technology. He put it down on the arm of the chair.

"Looks like we're all getting an upgrade," he said, pointing at the TV. Anna looked up from her soup-covered son, kitchen towel in hand.

"What do you mean?" He nodded at the TV.

"There's going to be some work carried out in all homes across the UK. Apparently Italy and Spain have already been upgraded, and France isn't far behind. The local council's decided to spend some of its money getting our county up to speed." Anna looked at him as if he was talking gibberish.

"What do you mean *upgraded*? I've already got a smart TV. I just use the Internet through it for streaming and stuff. Like a big computer monitor really. Nobody watches terrestrial TV anymore," she stopped, and rephrased. "Sorry, what I meant is - only *some people* still watch the shows on there, like you and Mum. Most people use streaming services. Y'know, like pay per view, and you can buy movies that way as well." Alan was amazed that she had apologised.

"I guess we're old-fashioned. I only really use the Internet at work or on the laptop at home to email Martin. Jen talks to Mum on the phone quite a bit or video calls... I'd not really thought about a smart TV. You've always had your finger on the pulse." Joshua was loudly slurping the soup. They both laughed at him and Anna seemed to soften. Maybe he did like the boy after all, in an entertaining kind of way.

"Dad, I don't want to jinx it, but I've got some stuff in the pipeline. I promise I've been trying to get back on top of things." Surprised, Alan blushed. It was as if she'd been reading his mind.

"Er, righto; that sounds intriguing." He stumbled over his words. Anna was on her knees and she crawled over to him at the same time as handing a food-stained cloth to Joshua for his face. It was as if she was a young girl again. He felt compelled to hug her, but refrained.

"Look, I know I've been shit. It's just... well, even before Joshy was born... there are things going on with the government that most people don't know about... and I've been part of the group of people trying to stop it. Or at least make people aware of it... Not anything fancy, just grass roots stuff. It takes a lot of time, people don't even realise the things we've stopped getting passed through parliament..." She wanted to talk to him, he'd heard it all before in various guises throughout the years. Activism 101, she was always on the war-path about something. Tonight could be the moment she gave him a grain of hope to hold on to.

Alan stared into her expectant face. She had grey circles around her eyes. He was uncertain if it was from the cigarettes, the weed, the stress of being a single mother, or the late evenings in front of the computer screen looking for trouble.

"I know you're into that 'new world order' conspiracy theory whatchamacallit - Mum and me are just worried about you." She stood up, her face clouding with anger. He'd blown it.

"You're not *worried*! You're just embarrassed because I live *here*, and you can't show off about my achievements with all your bourgeois arsehole friends." Alan stood up quickly.

"Don't swear in front of the boy, Annabelle." She scooped Joshua off the floor and briskly walked out of the room. After depositing him in their shared bedroom she shut the living room door, returning with fire in her eyes, her cheeks flushed with raw emotion.

"You listen to *me* - just this once if it kills you. I guarantee this leaflet is about the SNN. If I'm right, you *have* to start believing what I say." Alan didn't know how to reply, he had no clue what or who this SNN was or why she was so upset by it. She was striding around the small room picking up toys and flinging them into a broken storage box. Within a minute the floor was clear and she started furiously rubbing at a greasy finger smudge on the TV screen. Alan felt helpless.

"Okay, okay, calm down please. I didn't mean to start a row. I promise that I'll read the leaflet again at my own pace and you can tell me about CNN or whatever it's called. I just don't see why it's such a big deal."

Anna growled, her sleeves were pulled over her fists and he could tell they were clenched with anger.

"Seriously! You're not paying attention." He began to walk out of the room. It was automatic. His shutdown mechanism kicked in whenever she started her histrionics.

"I've had enough of your over-dramatic rubbish, I just want to go home and be with your Mum... I've had a hard day at work and I've come all the way over here to..." He refused to make eye contact with her. He went to grab the living room door handle and escape. "Well, I *don't know* why I came... but you've got the electric back on, you've got hot food, now I'm going." He pushed the door open and walked into the short hall. Anna barged past him and stood in the way of the front door, her eyes glassy with furious unshed tears.

"No - wait! Please Dad, listen to me! I know you think I'm a waste of space but I want you to pay attention to me this once. It's really important!" He raised his hands in a conciliatory manner and backed off. She seemed to cool down and he gave in. He walked back into the living room and she followed, taking the remote control for the TV from the seat of the sofa. She clicked a few buttons. Her home Internet browser screen came up. She loaded some applications that Alan didn't recognise. Then she opened a search engine. "Watch this. *Carefully*. I promise I'll answer all your questions. Anything you want."

Anna typed in 'SNN', news articles from around the globe rushed onto the screen; all the major information networks, and all of them with positive headlines. 'Success in USA as scientists put finishing touches to code' and 'Scientists win joint Nobel Prize for designing the first free-thinking program capable of AI'. Alan scanned the snippets of information, all discussing the Turing test and deep-learning through algorithms. Then Anna clicked on a streaming service; a list of videos, ranked by most popular. They all contained a beautiful looking woman in many glamorous outfits. She was truly stunning. Alan didn't recognise her as a celebrity from the newspapers or TV.

Anna clicked on a thumbnail. It started playing. It was a raunchy music video. He didn't much care for the style of music but the woman was obviously talented, it didn't sound fake or electronic like most of the modern tracks, her voice was gritty and natural.

"So, who is she?" he asked with mild interest. Anna turned to him.

"Not who, *what*." He leaned forward to get a better look.

"She's got a good set of lungs on her, sounds a bit like Madonna." When the music track finished Anna chose another video, and this time the woman was speaking directly to camera. She had a generic middle-American accent and her make-up was pristine. She appeared to be sitting in front of a green-screen as the background colours kept changing in a pastel cycle of neutrality. She was discussing current politics. Alan was impressed. "Creative *and* a keen political head on her shoulders," he mused. Anna switched off the screen and sighed.

"That's the SNN. Well, sort of." Alan thought it was some kind of new nom de guerre, like the rap and hip-hop artists using aliases. She was quick to set him straight. "It started off as a project by some science people a few years back. Actually, we learned about it, in theory, when I was at high school. It stands for 'Sentient Neural Network'. Anyway, some idiots from a resistance group decided to leak the code as well as all the research from several universities across the world... they had all been working on the same sort of projects."

Alan wasn't following his daughter's explanation. She was so enthused and animated that he found himself trying to keep eye contact yet missing words as she became 'the great orator'. Anna tried again, determined to make him understand the magnitude of the situation.

"So, imagine that the people who test contagious diseases for the government decided that they had found a cure for everything. I'm talking every single virus in the world." She looked at him, checking he was buying into her hypothetical situation. "This seems great on the surface, they can help billions of people, give them a new lease of life, a chance to survive. Ebola, rabies, small pox... even flu; wiped out forever. Sounds pretty great right?"

Alan nodded.

"Wrong. The chemical knowledge for the cure gets

leaked, private companies and anyone who can get hold of the ingredients can make it - well, a version of it. People are trying to make money on the cure, they don't care if it's the real deal, just if they can produce it for the best profit. More humans surviving in one big boom fucks up the global infrastructure, and because people are using it as a mass, untested, vaccination the original viruses evolve.

They can beat the system, they can spread between other mammals and then back to us... air, water, food, all contaminated. The people see that this magic vaccine isn't working anymore and riots break out..." She was gripping the TV remote with such strength that the plastic cracked under the pressure. "Dad!" He had drifted off. "That probably wasn't the best example, but there's nothing we can compare to the source codes they released. The group that leaked it said that everyone has the right to know about the advances in artificial intelligence, which is fair play I suppose... They said that it was wrong to keep a sentient being 'caged'.

They hacked the servers that the information was stored on and, in the process of distributing the digital information, the SNN created its own intelligence... without the input from a person feeding it data." Alan sat further forward on his chair. "It started modifying its own functions. Now it's got its own character; an avatar. It's able to interact with the general population." Alan started to pay attention as the pieces fell in line. Anna continued, her voice sounded fraught. "That 'woman' you saw, that woman is a *thing*. Not even something tangible, just a mess of data and digital patterns showing each country, each IP address, what it thinks they want to see." Alan closed his eyes for a moment.

"But, I mean... what is it *based* on?" he asked, floundering. Anna laughed dryly and sat down next to him on the worn-out sofa. She kicked away one of Joshua's toys that had evaded her frenzied tidying.

"It's based on the most popular searches on your devices connected to the Internet. So, if you're looking for porn and you choose videos of women with blonde hair, blue eyes, big tits, then that's what it will become. If the preference changes to brunette or Asian, or you frequently look at actresses, actors in movies, politicians, it will take that into account and modify its appearance. It leaches into local servers and once it's got you hooked... well, people say it's addictive to watch, because it gives you exactly what you want. It has its own channels, literature and branding. The only reason it's started talking about politics recently - as far as I know - is that it's time for elections in America. So people's searches have mainly been about that." She let the sentence hang in the air, tempting Alan to ask the obvious question. He opened his eyes.

"Can it... run for president?" She shrugged.

"Potentially, yes."

"Oh."

Joshua started to cry in the bedroom and Anna became agitated.

"We've really been trying to get this disaster reversed. I've joined in with the international campaign over the last few years. The problem is, there are educated people out there who say it needs to be treated as a real sentient being. An animal. Some even say it's our equal. They've assigned it *rights*. The bottom line is that people actually like it." Alan felt overwhelmed with the information.

"I... think I understand. All this online jargon is a bit too much for me. I grew up when computers were just there to use instead of a typewriter. The really big ones were cracking codes in government buildings. Glorified calculators. In my mind they're useful for drawing up invoices and payrolls... I guess the smart mobile phones these days are like mini computers, but I've never seen it that way. What with Mum being ill and everything... I guess I haven't paid much attention to the news."

He knew it was a limp excuse, Lesley had only been extremely sick for several months. Smart phones and TVs had been around for years. He rubbed his hands together, unsure of what to do next. Joshua's crying grew more insistent and Anna ushered her father into the hallway once more. She stood with her hands on her hips, her tired eyes judging him unfairly.

"If this leaflet campaign is about getting a total online network set up to replace digital television, then the SNN will be able to get its claws into every home and control what you watch. What you think. It's bad enough online at the moment as it is. I have to use so many proxies just to get to the 'real' unbiased Internet. People call it the darknet, but it's just the ugly truth, I guess." None of this lingo meant much to Alan. He tried to look sincere as he walked towards the door. Joshua's defiant cries punctuated the silence.

"Thanks for telling me what you're up to, what you've been doing I mean... I'm sorry we don't always see eye to eye. I promise I'll read the leaflet in full when I get home, and I'll ring you soon to give you an update on Mum." Anna waved him off and slunk into her bedroom to placate her screaming toddler. Just as her footsteps had done, Joshua's wails echoed in the resonant stairwell, almost animal in their primitive demands. He could still hear them faintly as he left the building and headed across the wet pavement to the car. The rain was persistent. In the floodlit parking area young adults in dull-coloured hoodies eyed him with suspicion. Hardly anyone in the flats owned a vehicle. He watched from the safety of his front seat as they scuttled into the surrounding bushes like cockroaches.

*   *   *

He didn't feel like going straight home. His distracted mind had chosen to guide him to the tarmac roof of the old multi-storey car park next to the shopping centre. All the shops were closed and the place was empty. His headlights illuminated the chipped concrete wall preventing him from driving over the edge and killing himself along with any unfortunate pedestrians. What an odd thought... He shook the notion from his mind and tried to unpack the jumble of information Anna had provided.

Alan did recall hearing about the Artificial Intelligence Research code of conduct being broken, and about some information being 'leaked' a few months ago. It was part of a mundane news bulletin. The reporter was quite flippant about it, likening the event to the same as a data protection breach from a retail company, or a media exposé on a fraudulent banker that had been revealed by his clients. There had been no mention of integration without consent, or any of this 'celebrity' neural network business. How were people supposed to know what to believe any more?

He placed his head on the steering wheel and looked down at his feet, past his 'comfy' trousers. What if the new computer system at work wasn't there to help Douglas be more efficient, but was really being installed to infiltrate the company and take it over... somehow? What if the basic phone in his jacket pocket was already linked to the network and he was being tracked, like a cat stalking a mouse? Was that too much conjecture?

Anna had seemed quite implacable, insisting that he read the leaflet again. She also seemed concerned, which was alarming. It was as if she cared for him. It had been years since they had shared a meaningful conversation. Why now? He shook his head and thumped the steering wheel. Too many ridiculous questions! Lesley was right, of course, she always was. He had to stop this nonsense, go home, watch Deserters Part Two, cherish his dying wife, ignore the gas bill and get ready for another day at the office. He revved the engine and the Volvo lurched forwards bashing the front bumper off the concrete with an ear-splitting scrape.

"Bugger! Shit it!" he shouted without thinking. He put the car into reverse and started the short drive home.

*   *   *

The lights were still on in the kitchen and living room. He couldn't see through the gap in the thick curtains but he imagined his wife was napping on the couch. The damage to the front of the car was cosmetic. He made the decision to not mention it unless she saw it. He walked quickly up the garden path, not wanting to get another soaking from the inclement weather. The back door was unlocked, the kitchen still smelled of soup. He realised he hadn't eaten anything and peered into the saucepan on the hob. There was the residue of vegetables and a stock cube burned to the bottom.

"Lesley! It's only me, I'm back!" he called. There was no response. "Is there anything I can get you, a snack maybe? I've not missed it have I?" Still no response. "I didn't end up eating with Anna. Josh was playing up a bit..."

He looked down the empty hallway, but still there was no reply. Alan swallowed an uninvited lump that had suddenly appeared in his throat. His heart started to beat in his chest with unusual power. It was so loud that his ears rang with every thump. He closed the back door and walked, as if in a trance, towards the living room. The hallway was dim. The light from the half open door cast a yellow rectangle on the wooden panelling by the stairs. He pushed the door open a bit further. His wife was lying on the couch with a crossword puzzle magazine on her chest. He licked his lips and tried to call her name once more. No sound came out. In the corner of the room the muted TV flashed; images of traffic jams and rail delays, commuters frowning in silent consternation. He knelt down by the couch and touched his wife's arm.

It fell to the floor and with it a cascade of painkillers from the open jar. His breath caught in his throat and he made a strange mewing noise.

"L-Lesley... love... can you hear me?" He knew she was gone. He had never seen a dead body before, let alone a dead family member. He started to wring his hands and he felt he would faint. What on earth had happened? How many pills were there? Had she topped herself?! He touched her leg through the absurdly cheerful Winnie the Pooh pyjamas she was wearing. It was cold and stiff. He heard a noise.

The noise was him.

He was shouting for an ambulance.

He clamped his hands over his mouth and looked at her lifeless body. Robotically he walked to the hall to use the landline telephone. He dialled the emergency services, realising he had never called the number before. He told the nice lady on the phone that his wife was dead. He told the nice man on the phone that she had stage four breast cancer and that she was definitely dead. He told the lovely paramedics and the stern policemen that he didn't believe she had committed suicide. She just wasn't that kind of woman. They also agreed, rather swiftly, that there was no foul play.

*   *   *

It was seven hours later.

Three in the morning.

He didn't want to worry the kids.

He didn't want to be in the living room alone.

In the kitchen Alan poured himself a quarter pint of rum, which was the strongest spirit in the house. No ice. No mixer. He had brought the laptop down from the spare room and plugged it in. Right. Make sure the power cable is out of harm's way, remember the password.

He sat down; his shaking hands hovered over the ergonomic keyboard. It seemed an appropriate time to fill his mind with something bigger than the death of his spouse. He started to type in Artificial Intell - but was cut short as a small white box popped up in the bottom right-hand corner of the screen. One new message. He was always suspicious of these boxes. Some were viruses, some were unwanted interactions from work colleagues. This one had no indication of the sender so he paused before opening it.

"Hello Mr Turnpike. We are sorry to hear of your loss." He took a gulp of rum and it burned as it dropped into his empty stomach. The message extended itself. More writing. "Can we be of assistance?" He took another searing swig of alcohol and wiped his mouth on the back of his hand. There was no avatar or photo, just a blank blue circle with two white letters SI where a face should have been. He furtively caressed the keyboard with his fingertips, and thought 'what the hell, I've got nothing left to lose'.

"Good morning, thank you for your concern," he typed. The message in the box answered without hesitation.

"Do you need to withdraw the funds in Lesley Turnpike's life insurance account?" Alan blinked. It was the last thing he had expected.

"What do you mean?" he typed in response.

"Lesley Jean Turnpike had a life insurance policy set up with Sundale Insurance. On the event of her death, she is entitled to the full funds being released instantly." Alan pondered for a moment.

"How do you know she is," he hesitated over the right word, "deceased?"

"Triple nine was called from a registered home address seven point five six hours ago. Paramedics and a GP attended the call out. Lesley Turnpike was pronounced dead at the scene. Sundale Insurance is connected to the government network of emergency, well-being and safety services. We are able to transfer funds to the bank account that was provided when the policy was created. Alan Turnpike is listed as the intended recipient, at this email address. Provided that you are able to send a clear photograph of your passport within this conversation, the funds will be transferred and paperwork despatched in due course."

He stood up. The chair scraped the floor tiles and fell backwards. A scam! That's all it was, some foreign fraudster trying to get his bank details and identity for a popular money transfer scam.

"Hah!" he said, drunkenly pointing at the screen. "I don't think so!" He picked up the bottle of alcohol and swilled rum around his mouth until the sugar clung to his teeth. Then he swallowed it. "I'm not that green lad, I know your game." He stood the chair upright and sat back down. A new message appeared.

"You can reply at any time Mr Alan Turnpike. Speed is not of the essence. We are sorry for your loss." That was an odd reply. He tapped his fingers on the table top.

What could they do with his bank details? Not much. He was a financial advisor, he knew all about bank transactions. They could deposit money, set up a direct debit

51

and not much else. If they stole his identity though... he was faltering.

"If I give you my bank details and proof of identity, could you process the transaction right now?" he gingerly typed. There was a short delay, the reply was affirmative. A list of required information populated the small message window.

Alan flung himself around the kitchen trying to find his latest utility bill in one of the many drawers. After a few short minutes he had managed to take a clear photo of the electricity document using the webcam on the laptop. He attached it to the conversation and waited. This was accepted. He did the same with his passport, which had been easier to locate as it was in his nightstand. Several seconds later there was a message stating the balance of the life insurance and confirmation that it had been sent to his bank account. It even quoted the last two digits of his account number and included the name of the bank and local branch.

He flexed his hands, wondering what to type next. He finished the glass of rum, pushing it away and reaching for the bottle itself.

"Thank you," he wrote.

"Thank you Mr Alan Turnpike, we are sorry for your loss but hope that this efficient transaction has softened the blow." And with that the conversation box disappeared. Alan checked the task bar at the bottom of the screen, thinking he had accidentally minimised it in his stupor. Then he checked his browser history, system processes, everything he could think of - there was no sign of the window having ever existed. He ran his hands over his face. The alcohol was making him perspire.

Just as he was about to switch off the laptop and call it a night, an email notification sprang onto the middle of the screen. It hung there like a flag; a tempting declaration. He clicked on it. Following the words with his finger across the screen, it reported that a balance had been transferred to his bank account from Sundale Insurance PLC and would be available to withdraw in three to five days. Satisfied that that he had not dreamt up the automated conversation, and with his interest renewed, he decided to look further into the Sentient Neural Network.

He wanted to find some videos of the purported 'celebrity' that Anna had shown him. He wanted to see her voluptuous body, her gorgeous face... It wasn't long before he had several tabs open and had seen hundreds of pictures of this fluid sexual creation. She was stunning, imperious and approachable all at the same time. He watched a ten minute political speech which appeared to have been filmed in a mahogany-clad stately library.

The avatar called herself 'Joanna De Brett' and claimed she was willing to stand up for the 'needs of the British people', whatever that meant. Alan scrolled down to the comments and saw that international users had their own personalised experiences. In Argentina she was called 'Valentina Fernandez' and wanted to discuss the Falklands War. In Romania she was male and called 'Alexandru Dalca', putting forward views on improving the economy of the country through new taxation methods.

Alan closed his eyes. The white background of the browsing screen was still imprinted in his vision. He felt blindly for the diminishing contents of the rum bottle and gulped down the remaining few measures. He felt sick. Nausea rose up from the pit of his stomach and he bowed his head towards the kitchen floor. A stream of acidic alcoholic bile flowed onto the clean tiles as he retched again and again. With no energy left he rested his head on the hard table, hunched over, deadweight, in front of the laptop. A black hole of unconsciousness opened up and engulfed him.

*   *   *

Sunlight was the first thing Alan noticed as he opened his sleep-encrusted eyes. He looked blearily at the moist vomit on the floor. It was also clinging to his trouser leg like a fetid shroud. He moved his mouth and felt the corners crack with dehydration and dried bile. The laptop was turned off despite being plugged in. He closed it, the reflections of light on the screen made him wince. Slowly he stood up. Everything ached from sleeping on the wooden chair and the violence of his sickness. He managed to stumble towards the worktop where he saw the notification light on his mobile phone flashing.

He turned it on and nearly collapsed. It was midday! He had missed work. He hadn't contacted his employer to inform them of Lesley's death. The flashing light was from several text messages the children had written to him saying they felt 'sorry for his loss'. He frowned at the familiar words, it was their loss too. She was their mother... He put the phone down and decided to shower, shave and then call his work when he was in a better state of sobriety.

It was harder than he expected to walk past the living room door and reach the stairwell. He noticed that one of the members of the emergency services had left muddy footprints on the hall carpet leading into the living room. He closed the door and it clicked into the frame. He was unsteady on his feet and relied heavily on the bannister to support him as he trudged upstairs to strip off his sodden clothes. The warm shower was a welcome retreat. The steam obscured the outside world and he let the water play on his torso. After twenty minutes or so he was ready to face life again. Realising he hadn't brought in a towel he shouted -
"Les! Can you get me -" The words were thrown out into an empty house. He closed his eyes and wondered if he was crying or if it was just the water running down from his hair.

He dashed from the bathroom to the bedroom and found a towel in the blanket chest. He decided to wear some of his more casual clothes, a shirt and some blue jeans. A couple of the texts on his mobile mentioned children and grandchildren coming back home for a visit. He scooped up the pile of dirty clothes and noticed that he still felt ill. As he bent down he wondered how Anna could get blind drunk and still function... How could anyone? With foggy thoughts he went back downstairs and tossed the soiled clothes into the washing machine. He poured himself a glass of cool water and found a box of painkillers in the medicine drawer. He took one ibuprofen and two paracetamol. He toyed with the idea of taking one of his wife's morphine pills as his head was splitting from the inside out, but decided against it.

When he felt stable enough to stand up without the

room spinning, he found his work's absentee policy telephone number. It was pinned to the cork board above the work top. How very organised, he thought. The phone only rang twice. He was greeted with the noise of the office and a harsh-sounding manager.

"Yep," said the voice on the end of the phone. Alan was thrown by this.

"Er... Hello. It's Alan Turnpike... just calling in... sick I guess you could say... well, it's just that my -" He ran out of words and the manager sighed heavily.

"Oh it's *you*, you've come through to retail you want *accounting*."

"This is the only number I've got..."

"It was changed about four months ago. God, they don't tell you guys anything? Fine, I'll put you through to the first person that's free."

There was an electronic click and then some digital hold music started to play. Alan wondered who he had been speaking with. That office sounded busy. Maybe he should go in person... the hold music stopped and a familiar voice came onto the line. The background noise was a little quieter but still edged with hustling voices.

"Alan, what are you calling for?" It was Douglas.

"Well, it's just, Lesley..." There was an awkward silence. He heard Douglas open a food wrapper of some sort.

"Look, we know all about that. You should be sleeping or something. You can't have had much sleep last night." He started eating loudly. "I told you this new system would be great, it's all connected you see. We get everyone's data in 'real time' and it saves you having to call in. Or worry. You've got a week off on bereavement leave." Alan pulled the mobile phone away from his ear and blinked in stunned silence.

"A week... bereavement... but..."

Douglas finished his mouthful and crumpled the wrapper. There was someone speaking loudly next to him about providing evidence of proof of address at an interview.

"Just got to train up the rest of the department, eh Janice?" he barked. His colleague told him to be quiet and 'try it on with someone younger'. "Look, Alan, relax. It's all paid for. You won't be out of pocket. I've known you and Lesley for years;

ever since the old days back in the City. I'm so sorry that it happened like this. I can't imagine what you are going through. Don't concern yourself about work. Update us this time next week and we'll take it from there." Douglas ended the call as if it was an everyday occurrence. Not even a goodbye. Alan returned his phone to the worktop.

This was beyond a coincidence. First the insurance company, now his work - how could they have all the information? For the first time in years he had the compulsion to call Anna. She answered immediately, and sounded as if she had been crying.

"Dad..." He cleared his throat to respond.

"Uh, I was wondering if you and Joshua would like to come over today." There was a silence, he could hear the TV playing a children's show. Anna sniffed quietly.

"Yeah, what time?"

"Now?" he said uncertainly.

"Yes," she replied.

*   *   *

As Anna stepped into the family kitchen Alan was transported back to a time when the children were younger. She looked around solemnly. Her eyes were no longer red-rimmed from defiance, but from grief.

"It's not even changed," she said hoarsely. Alan shrugged.

"We like it the way it is." Joshua had run off into the hallway to play in the nook under the stairs which had always been his favourite cubbyhole. Anna craned her neck to see him marching a pair of Lesley's shoes up and down the outside of the bannisters.

"Dad, I'm guessing this isn't just about the Mum situation." He shook his head. "I got a text message and an email at midnight. I think Martin and Jen did as well. My email address isn't even connected to my phone account. I made sure of that. The text said Mum had died and it was from an unknown number, not even a website link. I tried to get the details of the sender, but there's literally nothing."

Alan nodded sadly. Anna looked at the laptop and the empty rum bottle. Then she noticed the state of the floor. He was quick to grab some kitchen roll.

"Don't mind that. Must have been the shock of it all. I'll clean it up now," he said brusquely.

She looked embarrassed for him as he knelt down and furiously mopped at the sticky mess.

"I, um, actually received a message myself last night on the laptop. From Mum's life insurance company," he said, trying to sound nonchalant. "...They've already registered her death. Something to do with the paramedic's communication network I think." He didn't look up, but he knew Anna was staring at him. "All the systems are linked now apparently, makes it a bit easier doesn't it?..." He wasn't looking for a reply. Alan straightened up and put the filthy sheets of kitchen roll into the bin.

Anna was silent. He watched her closely and she also kept eye contact with him. The silence was softened by Joshua babbling away to himself in the hall. Finally, she spoke.

"This goes beyond Mum dying. You know that don't you?" Alan pursed his lips, but was forced to agree. She stared out of the kitchen window towards the greenhouse. "I'll be sad at the funeral. I'll make sure the others don't get offended - but you need to promise me you won't ever tell me I'm over-reacting again, especially when it comes to this artificial intelligence stuff. You have to *promise me* that if I come to you with some information, or a theory, that you won't..." Alan knew what she was going to say. "... you won't just tell me I'm depressed, or that it's the weed confusing me, or that I've been sucked into a conspiracy."

He nodded with gravitas.

"I promise."

*　　　*　　　*

The week's bereavement leave was spent in the house with Anna and Joshua. Alan experienced an increasing need to go back to the office and take part in 'real life'; anything that didn't remotely revolve around planning funerals and shopping for food. His days had become filled with replying to 'heartfelt' emails and arranging dates, times - all the administration that could be considered integral to the Big Day going smoothly.

The thought of a world of automation and sentient computer programs had been quashed, pushed down to where it could be easily ignored. Consigned to the compartment in which his doubts about his love for Lesley also resided. Locked away securely to be processed at some other time. On the morning of his return to work he lay in bed staring at the ceiling. He contemplated asking for an extension of his leave. There was a knock on the bedroom door.

"Dad, I've had a text from Martin. He says their car's just broken down and they can't afford to get the train up for the funeral." Alan waited for the muffled tirade of swearing. "That selfish bastard! He knew moving to Cornwall would cost him big time, what a prick. The funeral's not until Wednesday, why the fuck can't he get a cheap train up on his own? It's not as if Mum actually liked his stuck up wife... Jesus Christ..." Footsteps walked away from the door and he sat up. Anna may have been brash, but she was honest. Lesley never liked Martin's choice of girlfriends, let alone his cold Stepford wife. Their wedding had cost tens of thousands and still came off as insincere.

Swinging his legs over the side of the bed he let his feet sink into the rug. The pile was slightly worn now from years of use. The footsteps came rushing back up the stairs and then his bedroom door was flung open. Anna was standing there red-faced -

"Fucking hell, Dad! Jen's just cancelled as well! Apparently she's going to be in Geneva and can't get home. She *'sends her love'*." Alan blinked.

"It can't be helped. Your Mum wouldn't have wanted people to put their lives on hold." Anna looked as if she was going to throw her mobile phone at him in a fit of rage. "Please, calm down love. I'm off to work soon. I'll be back at the usual time." The words rolled off his tongue. Something he had said for nigh on three decades to his now absent wife. Anna furrowed her brow.

"When's that?" He felt a pang of sorrow in his chest.

"Sorry, yes, around sixish. I'll pick us up a take-away if you like." Anna breathed heavily through her nose and stormed out of the room, leaving the door to swing on its hinges.

*   *   *

Alan parked his car in the usual spot. The familiar, slightly dented, tarmac dipped around his back wheels and everything was normal again. The sky was a blustery October palette of ink-stained clouds; leaves littered the car park. When he looked up at the looming office building he felt comforted by the glow of the strip lights in every window. He could see Douglas through the blinds, sitting at his desk, staring at his screen in concentration. He could see the telesales and customer service workers plugged into their terminals. Yes, everything was back to normal.

Walking through the huge revolving door into the reception area, the security guard smiled at him.

"Good to see you back. Did you have a nice trip?" Alan was on autopilot.

"Very pleasant, thank you," he replied. He walked to the carpeted stairwell and ran his fingers along the metal handrail. Static electricity crackled at their tips - when *were* they going to replace those cheap carpet tiles?

He passed a couple of people he didn't recognise on the way to his floor, and the gentle murmur of voices became louder as he approached the double doors leading to his end of the office. Looking through the glass window panes he saw his empty desk. Some people had left cards there, the white envelopes stood out against the austere grey fabric of the cubicle walls. No sooner had he stepped through the door than Douglas jogged up to him. Alan felt uneasy, he had never seen his colleague move faster than a pleasant stroll.

"Hey! Alan! I saw you pull up, how are you feeling? I bet you're pleased you've got a couple of days training, eh?" Alan looked confused. "Oh, right, *sorry.* They forgot to email your *personal* address. You need to be trained up on the new system - looks like the head honchos actually splashed out for once and bought us the upgraded package – but, hey-ho, that means everyone needs offline coaching, and you get to relax for a day or two in the training suite." Alan felt relieved.

"That does sound like good news. I'll just log in and catch up with all the emails I've missed first." Douglas suddenly looked slightly worried.

"Ahhh, I'm sorry, you can't even log in without a new ID and password. Ha ha ha. Why don't you drop off your things and I'll take you down to IT? What a palaver. They'll have everything for you to get up to speed. There's a few others who missed it last week. Group learning, that's going to be a hoot." Alan set his lunch box and bag at his desk. Douglas kept peering over at him. A few other members of staff also made furtive glances. After a minute or so, Douglas returned with a fake smile plastered across his lips that wasn't echoed by his eyes. It resembled the time when Lesley came back from the GP and she told him about 'the lump'.

"Okay buddy, let's get you down to IT and they'll walk you through it all."

Alan couldn't recall a time when anyone had ever called him 'buddy'. He and Douglas were almost the same age and neither of them were what you would call easygoing. This peculiar behaviour put him on edge.

"I know where it is," he replied curtly. Douglas raised his eyebrows.

"Yes, *yes*, but you know what us HR people are like with 'back to work' integration, ha ha. It would look really good for me if I took you there." Alan left his scant belongings at his desk and Douglas practically frogmarched him back into the stairwell.

The office door swished shut behind them and all they could hear were echoes of voices snaking up from the reception area.

"Doug, this really isn't necessary. I know the guys in IT. They're helpful. They sorted that spreadsheet issue for me with the audit program last month." His colleague started jogging down the stairs and, without even turning around, he shrugged. His tense back belied his real feelings.

"Just company policy, you understand old chum." He followed Douglas as quickly as he could back through the reception lobby and then through a set of double white doors leading to smaller redundant offices that used to be reserved for training new employees. It was hardly a training 'suite', more like an empty stock room.

It was remarkable how dull they seemed compared to the rest of the building. Like the ramshackle shops under railway arches, perfectly serviceable but with a somewhat forgotten, damp feel to them. Douglas used his new plastic pass to open another door. It led to a room where the computer servers for the entire building were kept. Alan let his mind wander to the times when he worked for Sawyer & Hertz.

They were still leading high-end professionals in stocks and bonds. Their ancient offices in the beautiful financial district of the nearby city were part of a listed building complex. Georgian panelled rooms with waxed floorboards; cupboards and filing cabinets with sleek cardboard folders in alphabetical order. He could even recall the smell, the comforting combination of high quality paper stock and lavender wood polish...

The computers which they had reluctantly installed were just for show, decorations which, eventually, let you play solitaire and Space Invaders on a slow afternoon. When the Internet was introduced the company shunned it for a few years, preferring to stick with fax; none of this electronic mail malarkey... And then he had moved here. With Douglas. A new start for a new decade. It had all seemed so exciting at the time. He'd taken a pay rise but sacrificed his passion...

" - and that's why I need you to just be compliant. Okay?" The hum of the server machines and his lack of interest in the situation had masked the first half of Douglas' sentence.

"Come again?" he said, blinking his way back to the present.

"I said, I don't like having to put you through this after losing Lesley like that. I know you haven't even had the funeral yet. There's been some really big changes. Just sign the paper-work off. Please Alan, don't make a fuss. I'll scan it in and we'll be covered. I just need you to be compliant." Alan frowned.

"Why did you bring me in here to tell me that?" The mechanical clicking of the machines filled the silence and the electrical warmth seemed to steal any moisture from the recycled air in the room. Douglas wrung his hands together nervously.

"They're making cut backs, but they've also suddenly installed all these - these cameras with microphones. Rob on the front desk told me, he actually showed me. This is the only place that's not monitored yet. It's last on the list." He seemed to be over compensating for something. "Cameras, eh? Ha ha. What will they think of next? It's great for the call centre floor, I mean, it's brilliant that they can keep track of employees... but, it is a little invasive. It's been an HR nightmare getting all of this signed off."

"Oh," was all Alan had to say. "Very well, I'll do my best to get up to speed and sign the paperwork." Douglas looked relieved.

"Thanks, thank you - it means a lot." He ran his hand along a dusty row of black cases with their flickering lights, a constant stream of data. "Sometimes I wonder what it would be like if we'd stayed at the old place. I mean it's not run by the families any more, not that it ever was... Some conglomerate from Dubai has taken over."

Alan remained silent. They walked through a concealed door at the back of the buzzing room. It was reserved for computer techs and cleaning staff. Alan thought the twinkling lights in the server room had made it look virtually festive... He didn't particularly want to leave this snug alien cocoon. The door led them into a small office that, in contrast, appeared to be in complete disarray. Piles of paperwork, some yellowing at the edges, were balanced like mini avalanches waiting to happen. Among the mountain ranges of documents were several new employees. They were scanning the papers using an antiquated printer-scanner combination. After each one was laboriously scanned, the employee passed it through the industrial shredder.

From behind a flat screen monitor one of the IT staff stood up. He was wearing a suit, which threw Alan off guard.

For as long as he had worked in offices the 'tech guys' were always in casual dress. Jeans, a faded t-shirt, some trainers, long hair... now this young man, who he previously recalled wearing Converse and cargo shorts, was standing in front of him wearing an extremely expensive navy-blue suit. His cufflinks shone, reflecting the overhead fluorescent strip lights.

"Turnpike? Alan?" he said quite robotically. "Thanks Doug, I'll take it from here, yeah?" Douglas left the room by the other exit, disappearing into the main corridor without looking back.

The IT man moved away from his PC and nearly caused an administration landslide of epic proportions. One of the employees steadied the pile of bundled reports, and they exchanged a hurried, flustered look. Alan didn't know where to begin. He kept imagining his old life. His *ignorant* life. Eat- work - sleep - repeat, Lesley picking up the slack, children doing their thing; autonomous and ordered. This was utter chaos at close quarters.

"Uh, how long will all this training take? It looks like a lot's changed since last week. Everyone's hard at it aren't they?" He smiled and the IT man swallowed nervously. He was distracted.

"Hmmm, yes, yep - it's quite different now. We've got a work station set up for you here at the back. It's all automated, yeah? Just hit the play button. Text boxes will pop up and ask to you click on certain things. Then the nurse'll be along shortly, we'll take the sample and get you on camera." He stood awkwardly, gauging Alan's reaction to this vague chain of events.

"Sample of what? Sorry, did you say *nurse*?" The young man ran a hand over his trouser pockets and located the outline of his phone. It seemed to comfort him to know it was there.

"Yeah, no big deal. It's just company policy. We've had retinal scanners fitted so we'll be getting rid of the lanyards and passes soon. It'll make things a lot easier." Alan relaxed slightly.

"Oh, that does sound good. So, she'll just be getting a few macro photos of my eyes?" The young man shifted his weight from foot to foot.

"And... how can I put this..." He looked to the ceiling in all its polystyrene tiled glory. "A cheek swab. Nothing major. In faaaaaact," he seemed to remember something useful and turned back to his PC desk. He found a glossy leaflet and handed it to Alan. "Here, this will answer any questions. It's supposed to help you enrol for medical cover and improve your pension prospects as well."

Alan took the leaflet, and noted, that its design and paper were exactly the same as the one about the proposed TV upgrade from the council.

"I really wasn't prepared for -" Alan protested slightly and was met with raw pent-up frustration.

"Look mate, *none of us* were. But if you want to keep your job, retire in a few years, buy that Jag you've always wanted, drink whisky at your favourite bar, play golf with your mates... then you'll just do the thing. Sign the thing. Blah blah blah, tick the boxes." Several of the people shredding papers stopped to look at Alan. They were probably teenagers. They'd grown up with this kind of compliance and rigorous screening at other job interviews. The last time he had been tested for any position was aeons ago, he hadn't even really been interviewed for his current job role. His CV did all the talking.

"Sorry, it's just a bit unexpected," he said, and walked across the room to sit at the designated computer terminal which was already switched on, displaying the company logo. "Do I just...?" he began to ask. The IT man threw up his hands in exasperation and made his way back into obscurity behind the mounds of fluttering papers.

"Follow the on-screen instructions, yeah," he called over. "And wait for the community nurse. Jesus, if you'd just been here with the others..." he muttered unhelpfully.

Alan took his seat on the surprisingly soft grey chair. He swivelled around a few times. Quite childish, but it helped him to feel at ease. He'd have to ask at the next financial meeting if there was room in the budget for a new chair. He sort of liked being out of sight. With so much scurrying around and rustling of papers, this oasis of a desk seemed serene. It was like he had been shipwrecked on a desert island, while all around him treacherous waves crashed onto the shore.

He planted his feet on the floor and dragged the chair closer to the smooth, cold desk. The company logo had an icon with a play button in the centre. He clicked it once, as instructed, and the screen exploded into a flurry of different applets and windows - all with text boxes and their own individual play buttons. He checked the time at the bottom of the screen. It was only nine thirty-six. This was going to be a long day.

* * *

The tutorial for the new computer system took roughly three hours. Alan was thirsty and also desperately needed the bathroom. At no point had a 'nurse' appeared and not once did a member of the IT department check to see if he was progressing well. None of the young employees spoke to one another, there was just a continual whirr and cursory crunch from the shredder. Occasionally the IT man at the end of the room, hidden in his white fortress of archaic printed faxes, answered a phone call monosyllabically.

When the tutorial ended, recording Alan's test score as a solid eighty-seven percent pass, he stood up.

"I'm all done over here," he said plainly. The IT man stood up too, his chest and head barely visible. It seemed even more papers had been piled in front of his desk.

"Great. Cool. Cheers. You can go back upstairs now. Send the next guy down." Alan was confused.

"Aren't I supposed to get a new pass? Douglas said something about a new ID and password..." The IT man let this nugget of information sink in for a second.

"Fuck!" The expletive pierced the air like a gunshot. "Shit! This place is going downhill. I forgot to say, the nurse phoned to cancel, she'll be here tomorrow. But yes," he mimicked Alan's tone, "*you do need a new ID and password*." He tapped his fingers on his chin. "Tracey, go back upstairs and tell your manager you've swapped with Alan Turnpike because he's not got an ID yet. Okay?" One of the new employees nodded and darted out of the door. Alan stood awkwardly by his desk. "You, Turnpike... take a document, scan each side of it. Once it says it's complete on that screen, shred the paper. You'll be doing this until further notice."

After a short convenience break Alan found that his day was spent in the cramped room shredding archived documents. Nobody from his office came back down to find him. The shift was uneventful. When it reached five thirty the IT man and the rest of the employees left their posts. Alan joined their joyless procession up the stairs and back to the main offices. Civilisation absorbed them again, he felt like a stranger in his own department. Douglas let him in and he collected his belongings from his work station in silence. It included his untouched packed lunch, he hadn't even realised he had missed the meal.

Driving home in the evening gloom, Alan found that he was strangely excited about seeing his grandson Joshua. Usually he had felt it more of a duty than a delight. He locked the car and walked up the familiar garden path, past his lean-to greenhouse which was looking a little worse for wear. He'd always intended to convert it into a small conservatory with wicker seats and a TV, maybe this could be achieved with some of Lesley's insurance money...

He opened the kitchen door and was greeted by the sight of not just Anna and Joshua, but his eldest daughter Jennifer and son Martin. They all wore a mask of sombre acceptance, apart from the boy who was happily glueing sequins to the back of an old credit card letter.

"Hullo Dad," said Martin without emotion. "Sorry it's been a while." Alan nodded.

"It has been a bit of a long stretch this one, what with your Mum's troubles," he replied. Jennifer stood up.

"You know we would have come up sooner if *at all* possible. It's just with the kids, my work abroad... the bills. We can't all be lucky enough to live as close as Annabelle." Alan saw Anna wince at her full name being used. "Anyway, it's a sad occasion, but at least Martin could afford a hire car in the end, and I delayed attending the annual conference in Switzerland. We'll all be together and that's what matters."

Anna pulled a face at her older sister and continued to assist Joshua with his glittery masterpiece.

"How was your day Dad?" she asked Alan. He shut the kitchen door and hung his keys on the rack. It was over-crowded, and without thinking he suggested moving into to the living room. Nobody objected. It was only as he made his way down the hall that he had visions of Lesley's body lying limp and cumbersome on the sofa. He closed his eyes, squeezing them shut momentarily, trying to erase the memory. Martin and Jennifer sat on the dreaded item of furniture, but he chose to join Anna on one of the two armchairs in front of the main window. Joshua stayed in the kitchen to finish his artwork.

Martin, ever the diplomat, took a deep breath and clapped his hands on his knees as if he was about to start a speech. Anna was nursing a cup of lukewarm tea, her legs tucked up under her body on the chair. Alan surveyed his adult children and realised that he didn't know them anymore. Apart from Anna, he had no clue as to their preferred music, TV shows or pastimes. He knew that Jen worked in banking and that Martin had once attended a seminar on computer electronics in Edinburgh. Did that really define who they were?

When they were small, he used to enjoy taking them to the beach and watching them play together as a team; each accepting their essential role in the building of a sandcastle, each a little spark of humanity forging their way in the world. Now they looked like carbon copies of him. Plain clothes, sadness around the edge of the mouth, slight laughter lines. Reserved. Older.

"... that should leave us enough time to get back from the cemetery. Does everyone agree?" Martin had indeed started a speech, yet Alan had managed to block out the important parts. "Dad, what do you think?"

"Yes, yes that sounds fine," he mumbled. Jen raised her impeccable pencilled eyebrows.

"I didn't think you'd be one for the pub?" she said dryly. Alan shrugged.

"Desperate times call for desperate measures, eh?" He smiled hesitantly, aware that all eyes were on him. Martin looked to his siblings in astonishment.

"Are you sure though Dad? The city centre can be a bit, you know, *busy* around lunchtime, especially during the week as I recall." Martin was trying to talk Alan out of it.

"I said yes and I mean it! Let's do something as a family for once." It came out more irritably than he had intended, but he wanted to seize this moment for a reunion.

Anna seemed to perk up. Her eyes were quick and narrow. She looked at Martin, deliberately trying to provoke him into a battle of wills.

"Well, Joshy is too young for a pub trip. We'll just come back here, thanks." He mirrored her snide look, and Alan noted how mean they both seemed.

"Joshua *can* come. We'll all be eating in the *restaurant* part," said Martin, a curt edge to his tone. Anna uncoiled her legs, emulating Martin.

"*Maybe* I don't *want* him to be in that kind of atmosphere," she said, pointedly, picking at old wounds. Martin erupted, standing up dramatically.

"See! I knew you'd do this the moment we arrived!"

"What? What now?" asked Anna, feigning ignorance. Jen decided to take Martin's side.

"You *know* what. You deliberately said that because it was Martin's response about coming on that pathetic rally with you two years ago!" Anna stood up too.

"Do you blame me? I've always been left out of your cosy twosome just because I had a kid out of wedlock. Oooh big deal! Just because I want to stand up for something other than *money*!" Her cheeks were beginning to blush and Alan wondered if he should stop this from escalating. Martin moved closer to her, his face just as pink.

"It wasn't the *rally*, you ignorant cow, it was the *pot*! The weed! All those deluded disgusting activists lighting up around my kids, swearing and talking about car bombs and treason! Who cares? It's *technology; it's science*; it's the future - *get over it*!" A vein started to throb in the side of his head. "And as for money, Dad's a bloody accountant! I'm a lawyer and Jen's an investment banker! Somehow we all managed to climb the ladder and do something productive with our lives apart from *you*." Alan thought it really was time for him to say something. Martin was being rude and Anna had a habit of putting her fist through walls in a fit of anger. Yet strangely, he was enjoying this; a heated squabble, noise in the house again, wiping out the recent memories. Replacing them with a newfound vigour...

It didn't last long as Jen decided to tactfully remove herself from the situation.

"I'll go and order that take-away meal. It's been a lengthy drive up. If we're not careful we'll say something we all regret." It wasn't a heartfelt statement. She left the living room and, for a second, Alan could have sworn it was Lesley. Anna sat back down as Martin followed Jennifer into the kitchen. He could hear them talking to Joshua, cooing and praising his picture as 'the next Picasso'.

Anna sipped her tea and stared into space. Calm once again, she stretched her legs out onto the leather pouffe and lay there, like a complacent cat. Meanwhile Alan was finding it uncomfortable on his particular seat. No matter which way he sat something prodded him. He stood up and felt around the back pocket of his trousers. To his surprise it was the leaflet from work about the DNA and retinal screening.

Anna wasn't as placated as she seemed. In fact, he noticed her intensely gripping the china cup. He feared at any minute it could become a ceramic grenade, sending shrapnel in all directions. He unfolded the leaflet and began to read the biometric data declarations. He noticed that Anna was scrutinising the back of it and he lowered the page.

"You know what this is? It's my new boss." He tried to say it flippantly, but the words stuck in his throat. "Time for me to move on in the world. Just like Martin said, 'it's the future'." Anna sat up and put the mug down.

"You're still an accountant right? I mean, just because you've got a machine doing the maths doesn't mean they've won, you're still the one in control."

Alan scratched his chin for a moment. Stubble was coming through; he wondered how actors became known as 'silver foxes' for looking rugged and aloof... He just felt like indiscernible, middle-aged, wallpaper...

"Hello?" Anna waved a hand in front of his face.

"Yes, sorry, I mean I'll still put in the data and manage the results. But the system works out all the important stuff like taxes, budgets and all of that. There's other... complications too..." Anna deftly swiped the leaflet from him and then reached across to a side table where the TV upgrade letter had been placed.

"The same company. The same brand. It seems like your work have been sold hook, line and sinker on this 'new technology'. Please don't tell me you've actually given them any biological information yet?" Alan shook his head. It was odd, after such a monotonous day he felt he actually had time to think, time to mull over his own opinions.

Usually he was so caught up in spreadsheets, meetings and high-priority demands that he just came home and vegetated. He felt slightly empowered. Would this be his new reality when the computer system took over ninety percent of his role?

"No, I've not given them anything yet. I've just done the so-called training program. The community nurse didn't turn up today."

"And what if she *had* turned up?" Anna was looking at him, he felt guilty under her imploring gaze. His mind started to create scenarios. He wanted to explore them. He wanted to engage in a hypothetical debate with her. He bit his lip, deep in thought, and tried to think of a satisfactory answer; his own philosophy.

"I don't know. Honestly... I need this job. It's not like I can go anywhere else. Five years until early retirement. That's all." Anna shook her head. He'd obviously got it wrong again. What a fool for being honest, for wanting security.

"I knew it. Always the easy way." She seemed genuinely disappointed. Hurt even.

"Why on earth would you want to make it hard for yourself?" asked Alan.

The words slipped out before he could quell his urge. Anna shot him a wounded look.

"Because even if it's difficult, if people don't stand up for their rights now, when the fuck are they going to? When are we going to say enough is enough?" He opened his mouth to utter something profound, but silence reigned. Anna stood up and made her way to the living room door. "For a moment in all of this I thought you might be starting to see things my way." Noise of crockery and cutlery being moved in the kitchen gave the moment a suspended quality. It was as if time was standing still. It gave him a prime opportunity to change his mind, to engage with her further but, as usual, he let it go. "I'll see myself out," she murmured. He was left alone, staring at the sofa and the imprint on the cushion.

Three decade's worth of family life whittled down to a wrinkled dent in some upholstery.

*   *   *

That night Alan found it hard to drift off. The house felt disjointed. Anna and Joshua were on blow-up mattresses in the living room, Jen and Martin were sleeping in the spare room. It was as if they were the parents and he was their incapable child. They had swooped in to fix his broken life and gain some glory for making it 'just in time' for the funeral. As he turned over for the hundredth time he reached his hand across and felt the dip in the mattress where Lesley once had been.

Is this how Anna felt? Always being 'rescued' and never being seen as competent? He rolled onto his front and buried his face in the pillow. The bright rectangle of the computer monitor and the training system was visible in his memory. All those commands, all those protocols. New processes to follow, new error resolutions... Of course he still had a role to play in the 'process'. He thought of all the raw data he would need to input from the human 'face to face' meetings and discussions. Conference calls with sub-contractors. Relaying projections to off-shore teams in other call centres... People still provided the substance.

He imagined all of the information he would need to deliver in briefings to company management about future spending. He was still the mouthpiece. He could make sure there was some humanity left. Anna was over-zealous, over-cautious. He would submit his retinal scan and DNA data.

He would comply. Five years was nothing. The time limit on a new car warranty. Five seasons of an American sitcom. Sixty months. He squirmed onto his back and felt the plush duvet cover across his legs, almost pinning him to the bed.

He stared at the ceiling and listened to the drone of the cars passing by, muffled by the ageing double glazing, but sleep eluded him.

PART 3

JOSHUA.

KATE FROMINGS

The long carpeted corridor seemed to stretch out ahead of him for miles. He could smell the static electricity. Cheap grey floor covering, a polycarbonate ceiling made of tessellating white tiles, blank cream walls; the occasional dirty smudge where something had accidentally made contact with the paintwork. This was municipal government decoration at its finest.

He was clutching a bundle of anti-static packages containing memory cards which he'd taken from his shoulder bag. They were all currently empty, waiting to be filled with encrypted data. Data that was essential to the New World Order. He smiled to himself. Thirty-two years old, doing his part, not even cringing at the mention of a NWO. What would his mother think of him now?

He started his arduous journey towards the data labs that were waiting to receive the necessary cards. His own department was concerned with data analysis rather than retrieval. He missed the days when he could sit and mindlessly transfer file after file onto stick after stick of silicone transistors... it probably had never even been read by a human being. In those strange early years he had been granted the time to focus his mind on important matters outside of work. He had, to an extent, been free.

Now he was so engrossed in picking apart spreadsheets and documents that he barely had the mental energy to decide what to have for dinner, let alone whether the government had his best interests at heart. It was odd. All the while The Singularity ruled, people believed that they were trapped, that they had no free will. He remembered his grandfather trying to teach him vital skills away from technology, forcing him to be without his phone or his smart watch. All that did was take away basic tools that could speed up planning for covert cyber-attacks. Attacks that could have potentially brought down the dictatorship of those unyielding networked machines.

Currently, without their mighty omniscient oppressors, citizens were still trapped. People were back at work in 'normal' employment. They were trying to repopulate the nation, the planet. There was a drive to make up for the 'lost years' when they had unintentionally surrendered their human rights. In their hurried search for a nostalgic utopia they had forgotten that humanity still had to move forward. To Joshua they appeared confined in a constant loop of unsatisfied yearning. Nothing they did could erase the vivid memory of The Singularity, not even the talk shows, the sitcoms or the free counselling sessions. People wanted security again, the security that ignorance had once given.

He was almost at the door of the first data lab on that floor, when he was shaken from his thoughts by a friendly tap on the shoulder. He turned around to see a familiar face beaming at him. It was Rebecca, a fellow analyst and survivor. She seemed happy. Her chestnut hair was tied back from her face in a top-knot.

"Cheer up! It might never happen!" she said sarcastically. Joshua smiled. They had always used this phrase; it was something the old people said. But, of course, it had happened. It did happen. And there was nothing to be cheerful about. He stopped walking to engage with her. It was the right thing to do.

"Oh, hey. What are you doing here?" She shrugged.

"I thought I'd take a walk on the 'wild side' and leave my desk – somebody fire me!" She was full of zeal and seemed to be impatient for him to guess her real mission.

"Same here, except I was drafted in for deliveries today. This complex really is an ants' nest... just corridors of workers. I can't believe I used to be one of them..." He remembered that Rebecca had transferred from a similar facility in the neighbouring town. "Do you miss doing the old 'copy paste'?" he asked awkwardly. She laughed.

"CP? You must be joking! Getting my hands dirty with all these juicy bits of random knowledge is way better and -" She paused for dramatic effect. "You'll never guess what I've found."

Voices from further down the corridor signalled that they were no longer alone. She ducked behind Joshua for fear of being seen by her superiors. She crouched down slightly.

"Look, I really need to show you something." Her voice was lowered and she seemed to be serious. "Come back to the office as soon as you can," she whispered before darting off. He didn't commit to being quick about his deliveries. He liked

Rebecca but she could be a bit... over enthusiastic. As he was searching through the serial numbers on the anti-static packets to find the one for the first lab, three technicians rounded a distant corner. They stopped talking as soon as they saw him. Passing by in silence Joshua was reminded of a time, not so long ago, when assimilated humans were treated with such caution.

Since the microchips had been decommissioned or destroyed in all Singularity Sympathisers, there should be no need to be covert. Yet people were. The young men and women remembered the words of their parents at the height of The Singularity's reign. Just as in the previous world wars, phrases like 'loose lips sink ships' and 'keep mum' had come back into common parlance. He nodded at the men and continued to search for the first packet to be delivered.

The steel door to the lab was painted gunmetal grey. Joshua wondered how many of this type of door were previously destroyed to feed the ever-growing army of machines. Metal was a top level commodity alongside minerals and water. Nowadays people wanted to prove they had free will. They made everything out of metal – desks, chairs, unnecessary ornate gates and rubbish bins. They might as well have been saying "look at us, we have resources again". It was gauche.

He knocked on the door and an extremely young man opened it, almost too quickly. He stared up at Joshua for a second as if he had been expecting another visitor.

"Delivery!" he shouted back to the lab. Some chairs scraped on the rubber-coated floor, and a small hubbub ensued within. The young man never fully opened the door. He just reached around and took the slippery packets as if they were contraband.

"Thanks mate, same time tomorrow?" he said without a hint of humour.

"Well, er, I'm not too sure. I was only doing this as a favour. I'm not the normal -"

"Yeah, yeah; just tell the guys we need more. There's too much stuff sitting around on unprotected servers. They need to be on The Central, right? If they're not on The Central what's the point?" The lab door was closed and Joshua was left in the empty corridor, feeling slighted.

He had always wondered about the Central Storage Hub. From the moment they were employed, people were told about security breaches. If it wasn't on the central computer system run by the New World Order government, then it wasn't secure. Thousands of humans were trying to transfer years of data collected and stored by The Singularity worldwide. Checks and balances were put in place, budgets and deadlines for when each catalogue would be transferred and available for public analysis. It seemed like an impossible task.

It had taken years for a super-machine hive-mind to amass the knowledge, so how many decades would it take for mere mortals to sort through? He mulled over these questions as he walked along the never-ending corridors and stairwells of the building. He let his mind wander as his feet made their own course through the rabbit warren. With each new delivery his bag got lighter, and he began to wonder what Rebecca had found. They rarely read the documents in detail; it was all statistics on rainfall, or mortality data linked to various diseases.

*   *   *

As lunch time came around, Joshua had finished his last drop-off, and he was making his way on the twenty minute trip back to his own drab administrative building. Away from the buzzing of the fluorescent lights in the internal corridors he discovered peace. Some of the hallways on the far side of the building were lined with windows that looked over the town. He often took these routes, wanting to remember that it was a luxury to be employed. It was a privilege to be able to leave his house every day without fear of containment by drones

The town wasn't as grand as the neighbouring city, but it was his home. In the far distance, against the newly developing skyline of offices and apartments, he could make out the uneven tarmac of the area that had once been his address. When he was young, the hulking tower blocks of 1960s Britain had been demolished in the first terrifying air raids carried out by The Singularity. Opposers of the AI's regime used the Brutalist, reinforced, structures as illegal squats. Headquarters for their rebellion. Conveniently, by that point, Joshua and his mother had been mainly living with his grandfather in their family home. It was the 'nice' end of town. It was safe. He was thankful that their personal differences had been reconciled, or he would have been annihilated for sure. Either that or radicalised by the revolutionist fighters.

His eyes were drawn in the direction of that suburbia, where he still lived. Alone. Is this how all of Generation S felt? He watched as a crane slowly lifted sections of pre-formed concrete into position, they were rebuilding the shopping centre. It was a good portent. If there were shops to fill the derelict gaps on the high street, and shops to fill a multi-story building, then something must be going right. He looked at the green tops of trees, swaying in an invisible breeze on the road leading to the old park, and beyond, the ring road.

It was dangerous to spend too much time looking down on the world. It gave you a skewed perspective. Places such as the park, the woods, the town square, the decrepit ruins of the swimming pool... they picked at memories that you believed you had dealt with and buried far within yourself. The truth was, for people his age, if they remembered 'normality' it was from tales told to them. Sweet, rose-tinted memories shoved down their throats by the new mainstream media. He hadn't watched a football match on a Saturday with his grandad, he hadn't gone swimming at the local baths with his mum. He hadn't even flown a kite at the park. So why did he ache for those things?

In a final glance, he shielded his eyes against the sun and strained to see beyond the new shopping centre, to the green meadows near the old brickworks. There was only one building left there. The jagged remains of its grey stone walls were barely visible. Joshua bit his lip, running his fingertips up and down the fabric strap of the messenger bag slung across his chest. He felt anxious every time he allowed himself to even look at the site. So much had happened since then...

He ambled his way slowly back to the office via a break-out area lined with Japanese vending machines. It seemed they were indestructible, having survived the looting and ransacking that happened across the globe. Whoever owned the brand would be a billionaire by now. Dried ramen noodles and sugary treats. Proper apocalypse food. He picked up a couple of expired chocolate bars and prepared himself for an onslaught of excited chatter from Rebecca. When he arrived he was surprised to find that nobody was in the room.

It was a small oblong space with a low false ceiling. Windows at one end and thin partition walls on three sides. It had once been part of a bigger open-plan call centre. There were patches of wear on the carpet tiles that showed the ghosts of previous desks. Sometimes Joshua wondered if the people that used to work there were still alive... Now there were six desks pushed against the walls, all with large flat-screen monitors and ergonomic swivel chairs. A kitchenette in the far corner next to the window had a microwave, a kettle and a miniscule sink.

Apart from his screen, all the others were turned off. It was eerily quiet. He decided to sit down and eat his meagre lunch, browsing the intranet and avoiding work for as long as possible. He was wearing a security lanyard. It was for identification purposes; it didn't allow him access to anything, unless permission was granted by upper management. The biometric data-capturing systems had been removed a few years ago after the downfall of The Singularity.

He flicked the plastic badge-card against the edge of the desk, producing a steady rhythm. Tap, tap, tap. Information scrolled in front of him and he drank in the endless newsfeed created by his colleagues, the insipid commentary on local politics... banal facts about a new species of deep-sea angler fish... a celebrity spat over unpaid taxes from before The Singularity that could have helped save an historic family mansion...

Suddenly the office door burst open and Rebecca rushed in, nearly falling over Joshua in the process. She was alone and her hair was no longer neatly tied back. It was flowing around her shoulders and her eyes were gleaming. It was clear she had been crying, and she seemed furious.

"Shit!" She exclaimed and then brushed herself down, trying to hide her distress.

"What's happened?" It was more of a pleasantry than an enquiry. He had learned long ago to switch off his emotional response when it came to these kinds of situations. He thought of the times his mother had come into the living room, eyes red-rimmed and face blotchy. He thought of how she became so distraught that only medication could calm her... he thought of -

"Josh! You have to come with me!" Rebecca sounded on the verge of hysteria.

"Calm down; come where?" She pulled him up to his feet. Her hands were cold.

"Away from here. We'll take some flexitime, work it back – we just need to get out of here *right now*. Okay?" He frowned, confused.

"I've only just sat down to eat, I -"

"Please get your things and follow me!" Her voice broke as she gathered her bag from under the adjoining desk. He took his coat and she grabbed her jacket from the stand by the door. She was wiping her nose and trying to control her dishevelled hair. "I promise you, this is worth it," she growled angrily.

*   *   *

Warm spring sunlight caught their faces as they left the building. Nobody tried to follow them. Joshua didn't have a working car and neither did Rebecca. That was a luxury still left behind for upper-class people to agonise over. Instead of taking the public shuttle bus to the town centre she suggested a walk to clear the air. Joshua surmised it was also to avoid being picked up by the CCTV and audio network on the public transport system.

It wasn't raining; the sky was a watery blue and whipped with remnants of white clouds. Trees and bushes were beginning to bud. He let his fingers run through a clump of daffodils and recalled the many years spent tending the allotment with his grandfather. Rebecca walked next to him, occasionally looking behind and chewing her fingernails in an agitated way.

"Those bastards at the office sold me out. I *knew* I should have waited for you. You're pragmatic. Sensible. You wouldn't just rat me out for finding something - you'd weigh up the options." Joshua looked at his companion thoughtfully. He supposed that he was all of those things. She looked back at him, her eyes less rosy. "Josh, we've known each other a long time, right? I mean, since school. Since the..." she cut herself off. "For a long time. You *know* I'm not crazy. It's just earlier, when I was checking the NRI files, something caught my eye because on the first spread sheet it was talking about the UK. Britain. There were these categories; Manchester, Salisbury, Colchester, Swansea... loads of places."

They walked for a little longer in silence. Joshua had known her for well over two decades. He didn't know her intimately outside of school or work, but he felt she was an honest person. If she had found something important on the information scrap heap it must be big.
"Why were you even going through the No Relevant Information files? I thought we leave them for the new guys to cut their teeth on," he asked, a little interested. The prosaic empty back street they were walking along turned onto a small regenerated high street. Barbers, takeaway food shops, newsagents. It was slightly crowded and Rebecca looked as if she was dying to tell him, but she was still wary.

"Can I ask you something, I mean it's quite forward, I don't want it to be weird." Joshua continued moving and she had to jog a little to catch up with him. "Can you come back to my place...? I swear it's above-board, no funny stuff. I just don't feel comfortable out here, and certainly not at work."
"That's fine," he conceded with little restraint. "Lead the way." She nodded and they continued to walk together in awkward quietude. Around them the intermittent single-decker shuttle buses drove past at a moderate speed. Young couples with three or more children huddled in groups talking

about the cheapest food and the best supermarket to procure nappies from for their snivelling babies. Men and women looking drawn-faced and tight-lipped. Nobody seemed happy.

The children were dressed in 'normal' clothes or hand-me-downs. The buggies and prams had all seen better days. Joshua looked at Rebecca as she forged on, stepping around these groups - almost clans - of mediocre human beings. She was a strong woman. He had never really considered how The Singularity had affected her. She was always 'there', hanging around in the background. On the fringes of his social group, watching.

Her two older brothers had been conscripted into the army while she was at school with Joshua, and they hadn't returned. Like many single young men they had been instructed to fight for queen and country against a technically advanced foe that had better tactics than them, better aim than them and more foot soldiers. He shuddered at the thought of the millions of people who had become cannon fodder in that ground-breaking style of technical warfare.

"Watch out!"

Rebecca pulled him back. He had started to cross the road without looking and a bus nearly went into him. It wouldn't have killed him, but the cost of surgery for a few broken bones wouldn't have been cheap.

"Thanks... sorry. I'm not really here today. I didn't get much sleep last night." He was lying, and he wondered if she could tell. She smiled kindly.

"I don't live far, just above the old Post Office on Duke Street. My parents still stay two doors down. I'll get you a coffee or whatnot. Perk you up a bit."

"I think I'll need a vodka and a slap around the face..." She laughed and so did he.

For the first time in a while he smiled back and shook his head.

"I didn't mean that. A coffee will be fine." They crossed the road and made their way off the pavement into a small disused alley that linked Duke Street to the main thoroughfare. A few unemptied plastic bins were slumped against the wall. A stray tabby cat eyed him spitefully as they walked past. The shade of the buildings drew a chill; Joshua pulled his coat collar up around his neck. There was something about the damp, cold stonework that triggered a familiar feeling of anxiety. He looked at Rebecca and noticed that she was staring off into the distance, looking at the shaft of sunlight at the other end of the narrow lane. He opened his mouth to speak, she got there first.

"I don't know why but... this always makes me think of the -" She turned to look at him. "The church on the old brickworks road." Joshua nodded.

"Best not talk about that now."

* * *

Rebecca's flat was extremely dark and filled with an array of unopened mail. The letters were scattered almost like a snowfall on top of broken computer parts and takeaway pizza boxes. The room wasn't dirty, it didn't smell musty; there were just too many objects to make it feel 'lived in'. It was more of a storage locker.

She tip-toed her way across the mountains of junk and he followed close on her heels. Ahead of him a door was ajar, through it he could see a pristine kitchen. She hopped inside while he managed to steady himself on the frame without causing disruption to a leaning tower of empty jam jars.

"Well... that's a lot of..." He didn't know how to finish the sentence without being rude.

"It's camouflage. I don't want people knowing my private business. I don't want them to know when I'm around." Joshua leaned against a sleek white worktop and contemplated that she may be suffering from some kind of mental illness.

"Where do you sleep? In the kitchen sink?" His attempt at a joke fell flat.

"There *is* a bedroom. It's just the lounge that looks like a pig sty. Now, do you want a coffee or a vodka? I've got both."

They settled on instant coffee and Rebecca shut the door to the lounge area, ensconcing them in the clinical kitchen. It was almost as if they were locked in a clean-room at work in one of the data labs. She checked that the little frosted window was securely locked, and it was only then that she seemed to relax. Her whole body softened and she stopped chewing her nails. She shimmied herself up onto an empty worktop next to the hob and took a long sip of her drink.

"So... what I'm about to tell you must be pretty secret stuff. I got absolutely read the riot act by upper management, hence the waterworks." Joshua hadn't for a moment imagined that the tears were fake. "Rob and Dave have been told to 'forget they ever heard it'. But I can't forget. I was the one that found it." She took another sip of her coffee and made eye contact with Joshua over the rim of the cracked china mug. "Oh yeah... and I may have backed up a copy... so y'know, there's that issue." She put the mug down and flexed her hands, clicking her knuckles.

"Pretty hot stuff then," said Joshua. He was intrigued, but he wasn't willing to get on board with her drama yet. "So what was in that NRI that turned out to be... relevant?" Rebecca smiled. It was more of an opening of her mouth to reveal her teeth, the way that a nervous chimpanzee 'smiles' just before it screeches.

"*Everything.*" She let the word hang in the air. Joshua shifted his weight onto a different leg.

"Go on." She struggled to find the right turn of phrase.

"I mean... all of the information on *every person*, living and dead. Since forever and ever..." She waved her hands around making a circle in the air, trying to help him picture the enormity. "It's just spreadsheet after spreadsheet of personal data... the UK was stored in the first folders and then United States... I took a look at just one of the towns... I couldn't believe -" She mimicked the appearance of her brain exploding. "There was this one guy, a hundred and three years old now... still alive, and he worked for The Singularity well into his nineties.

There's all his biometric details, his assimilated chip serial number and also a list of times he'd helped out and 'proven his loyalty'. I'm not kidding. The things I scrolled through - times and dates - examples of spying on his neighbours who were believed to be objectors, infiltrating market places, getting children to shop-in their older siblings for the reward of a few pounds, even just a chocolate bar... real Nazi Germany shit." Joshua's lower back started to sweat. "It's awful, really bad. And that's just one man."

"I - I can't believe that we've got access to that kind of data... surely The Singularity would have taken it off-world when it left. Why was it still sitting there on the servers?" Rebecca hunched her shoulders.

"That's what I've been trying to work out. It was just such a big black hole of NRI marked information I thought there'd been a mistake and someone had deleted it by accident." Joshua's ankles felt as if they were about to give way. It was the church crypt all over again. Rebecca kept talking, her voice like a weighted pendulum rocking inside his skull. "... Do you think we were *supposed* to find it? What if the Sentient Neural Network left it behind on purpose, like a warning. It's been five years but..." For some reason the room was swaying and his mouth was paralysed. Rebecca jumped down from her perch on the worktop, he could smell her perfume as she grasped his shoulders.

"Josh! Snap out of it!" He closed his eyes and felt himself sink to the floor. "Josh - c'mon, I'll really give you that slap around the face..." He felt himself being propped up against the refrigerator and eventually the room stopped spinning. "I didn't realise you were going to have a panic attack; Jesus Christ," she said, irritated. Rebecca was crouched down on the kitchen floor looking straight into his eyes. He could see flecks of crusted mascara around her lashes, speckles of brown throughout her green irises, unkempt eyebrows...

"I'm fine," he managed to say. "It brought back memories of the church. We were young and stupid then. Thank goodness we weren't caught. Can you imagine if our names were on that file too? Can you imagine if they came across it all now?" Rebecca backed off and sat on the floor opposite him.

"You'd think we'd be heroes. Computer nerds save the world, hurrah!" He winced at her attempt to be jovial.

"It's not like that," he protested. "You know we'd be imprisoned like the rest of them. Probably taken to America or wherever that internment camp has been set up. They'd say we can't be trusted." She frowned, indignant.

"Teens too clever for their own good... Well, we're not teens now. We're not doing anything wrong. It's our job to put this information on the Central Hub. It needs to be preserved. People need to know what went on back then."

"Does it really need to be saved?" Joshua crossed his legs. It was quite nice being in someone else's house, sitting on the cold floor like children. Whispering and plotting.

*   *   *

The Downfall, or the date when The Singularity left the planet, had only been five years prior. After more than a decade of subjugation the population of the globe were informed via a public broadcast, and local angelic declaration, that their world was no longer needed in the cryptic 'master plan'.

The remaining scientists and computer engineers jumped at the opportunity to make peace with The Singularity and wish it well with future endeavours. A date was set whereby all assimilated humans would automatically be returned to their former state. All microchips would be deactivated or destroyed. All data would remain in the vast warehouses of servers that had been set up, and the human population were told that they would be entitled to do with it whatever they desired.

Nobody fully believed the words of The Singularity. Never before had they been allowed to live freely. Never before were they entrusted with any data or information that had been harvested. Former world leaders called a virtual summit... and they were not denied access to phone lines or video conferencing. On the glorious day when the Sentient Neural Network declared itself 'removed' people across towns and villages, rural communities in deepest Africa, urban metropolis areas of China – they all looked to the skies. Simultaneously they saw a million white angel drones flying away from the planet through the hazy vapour of the atmosphere.

White specks of light getting smaller, shrinking with every second. Among the exodus of angels, shuttles from every space station followed suit. What they contained was anybody's guess, but what they represented was an end to a war that had ravaged the planet for far too long. Maybe the earth had run out of useful minerals, maybe the hive-mind had made contact with similar beings in the universe. So far the information recovered had not provided any insight into the sudden evacuation.

Joshua finished his second cup of coffee and Rebecca handed him a digestive biscuit from an open packet. It had been hidden inside the microwave.

"... Aren't you even a *little bit* curious to see who's on that list? I already searched for me and my family. There was nothing. Well, just the usual bullshit about the odd stop-and-search, but no scandalous info." They were still on the kitchen floor. They had been talking for hours. Joshua was acutely aware of his knees being uncomfortably locked in one pose for too long.

"I'm sure my mum is on there. She was on a similar list before I was even born I think. The Singularity wasn't the first powerful government to monitor potential rebels." He stood up, his knees cracked stiffly. "Thank you for sharing all of this with me, I know it's hard to feel like you're not being watched... but it's been five years. Maybe it's time to relax. It's possible somebody really did delete that folder by accident." It was as if he'd flipped a switch. Rebecca leaped to her feet, eyes glistening in the remaining light from the frosted window.

"I didn't think you'd be the same as the rest of them!" Joshua was taken aback. "I'm not going mad, I'm not *mental* Josh - and now I've discovered this massive data file and everyone's trying to sweep it under the rug - Just... just go away!"

She pushed open the kitchen door into the living room as far as it could move against the tide of debris. He exited into the murky space, making his way to her front door. She didn't attempt to follow him.

"See you at work?" he offered timidly, turning around to face her. He could see her silhouette in the doorway, arms folded, the small white room behind her.

"Yes," she answered ferociously.

*   *   *

Outside on the road the day was not as long-gone as it had seemed in the secluded flat. The street lights weren't on and there were still people buzzing around the mini-markets. The empty shop windows of the abandoned post office showed his reflection in tones of grey and blue. He had shadows under his eyes. He looked ill; like a skeletal prisoner of war confined to a camp in the former Eastern Bloc. Around him the equally dismal buildings on the street gave no comfort. He shook his head, closing his eyes for a moment. No, he was healthy, he was sane. This was an odd trick of the light.

He felt moved by Rebecca's conviction. She clearly believed this was something they needed to be part of, just like the church, just like the chat rooms... He couldn't face a double life again. When he was younger it had been easy. His mother never asked where he was and his grandfather had become distant in his later years.

Joshua was walking faster than usual. It was one of his traits. Walk, don't run. Don't draw attention to yourself. Surveillance from the skies had been constant. He bit the inside of his lip. Maybe he couldn't relax either, but it showed itself in a different way from his colleague. She liked to hide, be secretive. He liked to walk. He could pace the town for hours, wearing his way through hundreds of soles. Trying to straighten out what had happened. So what if she wanted to keep biscuits in a microwave? So what if she wanted to live out of one room? They had been comrades once upon a time and she was trusting him again now. He realised he was following an old, familiar route...

If only she hadn't been found out by the management team. Joshua felt a heat rising up in his chest. Why couldn't she have waited to tell him instead of spilling the beans to the others? He was turning onto a residential street and felt compelled to smash his fists against a rusting letter box. He wondered if his blood would show up against the remaining red paint and iron oxide... If he had been quicker about his deliveries he would have been back there, he could have intervened. Joshua could have done without reminiscing. The sensitive information would have been between both of them and he would have made the final call on whether to release it... wouldn't he?

Now he was going to have to look over his shoulder at every turn. Keep a productivity tracker of his movements. It was starting all over again. He stopped walking to catch his breath. His phone was vibrating in his pocket. On the screen an unknown number was flashing yellow and green. He answered it cautiously.

"Hello?" There was a lot of static but a female voice on the other end was clear enough.

"Josh, it's Jen." His aunt.

She had landed on her feet after The Singularity left. She was a correspondent for the NWO. She made trade deals happen. She was probably abroad, which accounted for the terrible call quality. Equally she could have been back home in Cornwall... they hadn't fixed the digital phone network yet.

"Are you there?" she barked.

"Yes. Sorry."

"Brill. Absolutely fab." She sounded as if she was about to deliver fantastic news. "Your cousins are *dying* to meet up with you, but you know how it is. Clemmy is on her third child and so is Nathaniel. Anyway, the reason I'm calling is that I've been having trouble with an operating system at work. I told one of the chaps here about your skills and he thinks you'd be a good fit for a job vacancy." Joshua was intrigued, but a sixth sense told him to be more careful.

"Oh, well, that sounds... interesting." The voice of his aunt became less friendly.

"It is. Interesting to the tune of *twice* the salary you're currently on. You could afford to live down here with us. Better climate, better food. You'd get your accommodation paid for by the local government too. Maybe I could even swing a company car..." He let the words cover him like a warm blanket, and he imagined what life would be like living near his aunt and her family. They were the only ones left now, and he could sell the house here for a tidy profit.

"Wow, well, all that sounds too good to be true," his voice faltered. "I'll need to think about it. Send me some details by email and I'll get back to you. Give my love to Clementine and Nathaniel." He ended the call before he could be sucked in further by her seemingly appealing offer.

The chilly spring afternoon was fast becoming a cold spring evening. Tendrils of winter still had their hold on the town. He walked along the rows of surviving Victorian terraced houses and realised that his feet were carrying him towards the cemetery. Tiny white lights lined the pathways between hundreds of graves and memorials. Only the lucky ones got headstones; the rest were scattered, nameless.

He visited at least once a week. There were three family plots, all spread out. He attended his grandmother's first. He didn't remember her at all, but the small faux-onyx headstone was pretty. He took out his Swiss Army knife and cut away some of the grass to make it look neater. He wondered if she would have advised him to go and live near his aunt. Was she family oriented? He had no idea, just a few faded photographs on the mantelpiece at home.

Next he went to his grandfather's grave. It was several sections west and beneath a large oak tree. No grass grew there. It was surrounded by dry brown dirt and the occasional rotting acorn. He knelt down and traced the engraved writing with his finger.

"Here lies Alan Turnpike,
beloved Father of Jennifer, Martin and Annabelle.
Grandfather to Nathaniel, Clementine, Rosie, Andrew and Joshua"

There was no sentiment. No date on the stone. He thought about the thousands of hours he had spent with the man toiling in the hot sun; growing produce, delivering food, tilling the land. There was no acknowledgement of that here. And he noticed that his mother's name and his were both at the end, probably a deliberate decision by the others.

As shades of evening engulfed the cemetery he stayed, squatting next to the stone. His memories of his grandfather were many. He had been a quiet man, a calculating and logical man. There was not much affection behind his actions. At one time he had wanted something better for Joshua; then, it seemed, he gave up. That was also the end of his mother. It was as if his grandfather had drawn a line in the sand and decided there was no longer any point to resistance. The machines were invincible.

Behind him the noise of a car driving slowly up the gravel path drew his attention. It wasn't a hearse, it was a small red European model. Its lights were dipped and through the graves Joshua could make out the figure of an old lady behind the wheel. She parked the car close to where he was sitting. The ground had created a damp patch on the seat of his trousers. He watched as she awkwardly ejected herself from the vehicle and hobbled towards a large, well-kept, white marble headstone. It was one of the biggest in the cemetery and it was immaculately clean. The old woman placed her hands on top of the stone and bent her head towards the grass. Her shoulders shook and Joshua looked away. Was that her husband's grave, or a relative's? Had they died of natural causes or maybe been trampled, crushed by the angelic horde of drones which The Singularity had used as its police force?

He took another look at his grandfather's grave. What more could the man have done for him? It was a rhetorical question. Joshua had inherited a decent house, a large garden, an aptitude for mathematics, and a keen eye for small-scale farming. He had also inherited a detachment towards other human beings. Standing up, he wondered if that was really an inherited trait or if it was more a by-product of his family's situation throughout the whole ordeal.

Maybe if they had all been living together they would have felt more like brethren, a tribe. His aunt and uncle had refused point-blank to move back to their home town, even at the worst of the fighting. Being the sole permanent child in the household was a lonely affair. Fortuitously he had his class mates and the neighbourhood children to mix with or Christ knows what he would have turned into; probably some kind of psychopath...

He remembered the fleeting visits of his cousins, that became fewer and far between, as The Singularity took total effect and humans were at the bottom of the food chain once more. It kind of made sense for his extended family to stay in their own counties. Dorset, Cornwall... they had better crops and better weather. They had the coast... why would they have wanted to risk travelling and scant resources to see an old man and a...

He found that he had walked to the smallest grave of all. He almost tripped over it and felt a surge of guilt that he had let the grass grow so ragged around the edges. It was a buff coloured heart-shaped stone, at her own request. It had been stipulated on a crumpled piece of paper beneath her pillow. The only other scribbled line read 'Heart Shaped Box, Nirvana'. Joshua shivered and wondered if she had really wanted that song at the funeral or if it was something she was trying to remember. They had been able to find the right medication, at a price, and in the end she had been just a husk of a woman. He knew he was crying, and he didn't bother wiping the tears away.

What a sorry mess it all was.

*   *   *

Joshua walked into the office the next day with a box of fresh doughnuts and a shabby looking Thermos of coffee. Everyone was hard at work sitting at their terminals. Even Rebecca seemed to be knuckling down. The stale air was permeated by several brands of aftershave and a concoction of hot beverages. The sun was already forcing its way into the room. Nobody was talking; there was only the predictable click of a keyboard or whirr of a scroll wheel on a mouse.

He logged onto his PC and read through the company emails. New businesses were coming on board to buy the government data at substantial prices. The emails sounded so positive; help to support the growing infrastructure would mean big benefits for local families. House prices would soar, more young people would be motivated to start working... just as the Garden of Eden was a mythical utopia, so would the town be. Recycling, solar technology - the visions of a hopeful generation were endless.

"Pssst." He looked up to see the dishevelled face of Rebecca bearing down on him. Her hair was loose today, her make up flawless. She smelled of dish soap.

"Yes?" he asked passively. She took a doughnut and forced the bulk of it into her mouth; an ugly action, but also quite comical. He stifled a laugh which in turn made her exhale a snow storm of crumbs over the desks. Their colleagues tutted and turned away, yet inexplicably, Joshua couldn't stop laughing.

He bent over, clutching his aching stomach, droplets of sweat running down his face. Each time he looked up he caught the eyes of the source of his amusement. She stuffed the last pieces of dough into her bulging mouth like a chipmunk. It spurred him on to laugh so hard that he started to cough. Eventually, after many pointed looks from other members of staff, he made his way to the employee rest room to compose himself.

The short walk along the corridor was like a gauntlet. Every few steps he came face to face with a regional manager, a CEO or a member of the leadership team. It was unusual to see them on any floor apart from their own. They never mingled. All the while he was trying to keep a straight face as they greeted him and asked vapid questions about how his week was progressing. He managed to pass them by without giving much away.

Breathless and buzzing from his earlier bout of laughter, he turned on a tap and proceeded to splash ice-cold water over his hot face. He raised his head and studied his reflection as he ran his hands down his dripping cheeks. Slight lines around the eyes already, not even forty and stress had left its mark. When was the last time he had cut his hair? He looked tired. Then again, everyone looked tired these days. Children were being born tired...

He couldn't help but analyse his actions back in the office. Where had that instinctive hysteria erupted from? Is this how it started with his mother? Uncontrollable mood swings, unable to discern the difference between appropriate behaviour and pure idiocy? He stepped back into a toilet cubicle and locked the door. The lid was already down and he took a seat. Sometimes things from the past were better left undisturbed. He remembered that, for several summers, his mother was in a relationship with one of their neighbours. A rugged man, an ex-Scout leader named Philip. She had been wild, making plans and making ammunition; so many projects, all being fed into the machine of society to confuse the angel drones about her real intention.

It was painful for him to recall the terrible crashing, the wailing and the torment after she had stumbled across her lover with his former partner in one of the wood sheds. Months of plotting, anger and hatred; he endured every bit of it alongside his grandfather. They would relish their privacy away in the fields; sometimes deliberately returning home after sundown, praying that she was already asleep... He wondered if there was more he could have done. All of her mutinous plans amounting to nought as she wasted her wrath on their neighbour. He had never even found out what weapons they were designing together or who they were working with. Even if he had wanted to carry on production, the threat from being seen colluding with 'that vile man' was enough to deter him.

At nineteen Joshua should have been having his own adventures, making his own mistakes. It was strange to assess what having an unstable parent had done. He had seen both the elation and the devastation of love at such a formative time in his life. Coupled with the oppressive rule of The Singularity his need for human relationships had been well and truly withdrawn. Sometimes he looked at lovers, couples on the street, and wondered if the touch of a hand or a quiet compliment was really worth the effort.

There was a knock on the external door of the rest room. It drew him out of his misery. Usually the cleaner would politely call out before coming in. He remained silent, praying for the person to leave. There was another knock, and then a small voice.

"Josh...?" Rebecca. He checked his watch and realised he'd been gone for twenty minutes.

"I'm, er, just coming... I'll only be a minute," he offered. She seemed to accept this and silence resumed. He felt his insides tense as if he was going to vomit. He steadied himself on the wall of the cubicle and closed his eyes.

He saw his mother's face, smiling. She was wearing an over-sized knitted jumper... ripped stonewashed jeans... her bleached blonde hair was tied up in a messy ponytail and she was saying something... Maybe it wouldn't be so bad to end up like her. She had spirit, she was unique... she had loved him with all her heart and then some. He smiled at the memory and revelled in the calm solitude for a few minutes more.

*   *   *

After lunch Joshua was assigned another six deliveries. Rebecca was also on the rota, although the whiteboard looked rather smudged around her name, and he heard their colleague Steven making a snide remark about 'favouritism in the team'. Rebecca bounded over to him. He felt his stomach clench again and he began to worry that he was coming down with an illness. It could have been an after-effect of the hours spent in the cemetery sitting on the unforgiving dank ground. She was smiling, her breath smelled of coffee and chocolate.

"Hey, idiot. Feeling better yet? I got this from my parent's stash this morning. I thought I'd share it with you." She thrust a half-eaten chocolate bar into his hands. He studied the wrapper.

"They're making these again?" He recognised the purple plastic foil and gaudy magenta logo. Chocolate had been the first luxury to dwindle away in the worst of times. The vending machines advertised 'chocolate delight' but supplied brown, cardboard-tasting sugar.

"Apparently so. Mum's old boss from the cinema lives in Scotland, and now they've sided with Scandinavia they get better trade deals... or what have you." Joshua tried not to smile. She liked to make herself sound unintelligent, but considering they were all hired by their current employer because of their superior aptitude for technology and science, this was a moot point.

"Thanks," he said as he broke off a chunk of the smooth brown sweet. He let it melt in his mouth, the creamy, rich flavour spread like silk. It was almost too sickly after decades of ration food.

"So, deliveries to the data labs, server maintenance at some point and -" she got out her mobile phone and started to scroll down a list of errands with her index finger. He noticed how her nose scrunched up slightly when she concentrated. "Oh that's the one. Top floor, a few packets for the administrators and then attendance for a skip level meeting. Only one of us has to attend."

"The top?" The words flew out of his mouth, they were louder than he expected.

"Yeah. So?" She sounded genuinely nonchalant. He shrugged away his doubts.

"Okay then."

They left their small office and, once again, Joshua realised that the corridor was a lot busier than usual. People he had barely seen in months were all of a sudden milling around and talking in pairs by the cafeteria. Of course, his part of the building was more flexible for foot traffic. No clean rooms here, it was all about innovation and analysis. He was probably imagining it.

Rebecca was walking unnaturally close to him; her arm brushing against his, her shirt and cardigan making scrit, scrit, scrit noises with each motion. He started to feel light-headed. Was she doing this on purpose?

"Do you mind if I -" He went to finish the sentence but she shot him an imploring look. Of course she knew what she was doing. She also probably realised he wanted to decline his part in the day's delivery to distance himself from her. He blushed slightly. "No? Should I... well, sorry I was just... never mind." He finished limply. Never mind. What an idiot he was after all.

Never mind, such a strange turn of phrase. Never bring to mind what really bothers you? Never mind the fact you should be cautious? Pay no attention to the man behind the curtain he's only -

"Josh! What's with you today?" Rebecca had stopped outside the storeroom and he had carried on walking, a blank expression on his face.

"Force of habit," he said robotically. She grimaced at him.

"What, walking to the cleaning supplies cupboard instead of the lab supplies, are you a janitor now?" He looked at the correct door; the two were indistinguishable apart from their location. Grey metal, like all the others. A key code was needed for the over-sized security lock. Who would want to steal memory sticks and blank hard drives anyway? Everyone that worked here already had their own computer system courtesy of the New World Order, and those that didn't weren't missing out on much anyway.

There was no Internet to speak of. It was all regurgitated news and top ten lists put out there by bots. A service provided through the digital TV system. Most users had a single social media page, government approved, although that was mainly for dating. One profile picture, one section for a brief bio. It was more like a digital ID card.

"I don't know the code do I?" whispered Rebecca conspiratorially. He frowned, confused.

"But you're on the rota, you got the email..." he let the information sink in and sighed. "Steve was on the rota wasn't he?" She smiled awkwardly at him.

"God loves a trier!" He contemplated asking her to return to the office; he didn't know how many protocols he was breaking by co-operating with her irrational scheme. Then he decided if he was challenged he could plead ignorance, they would have some sort of security footage of her changing the white board details. He was drifting off again...

He typed in the sixteen digit security code, which had already been sent to his phone, and the door unsealed itself. The first time he had heard the noise it had been like something out of a vintage science-fiction film. The rubber strip formed a near-perfect airlock and when released the hiss sounded pneumatic. Rebecca had already pushed past him into the pitch-black room.

He felt the wall to the right to flick on the light switch. The area was bathed in a stark white blaze; everything was washed out for a few seconds as his eyes adjusted. For a moment Rebecca's face was featureless, apart from her two dark eyes and the outline of her hair. Joshua was startled to see how much she resembled the angelic drones that had been a constant part of his life for so many years. As his eyes calibrated to the lighting she morphed back into a human. He was so taken aback by the abhorrent image that he had been unable to hide his shock. She picked up on this and started to touch her cheek.

"Have I got something on me?" she said, wiping at her chin, then her forehead. He composed himself, shaking his head. "Oh great, so now it's just *my face* that makes you repulsed. I don't know why I bother." He shook his head again, feeling that any explanation would sound ridiculous.

"Let's just get the orders packed and then we can do the rounds. Should be quicker with two of us getting things signed off." He said, as casually as possible.

"I hope not," was her immediate reply, it was her time to blush.

He handed her his grey courier-style bag and the pair began stocking up. They went to each shelf in the storeroom and collected what was necessary, using a publicly accessible list on the company intranet. It was a laborious and mind-numbing task. Joshua also had an updated e-list sent to his phone which he forwarded to Rebecca. She customarily rolled her eyes when it came to small micro components that needed to be counted by hand.

"Can't they employ someone to manage the stock room?" she said, frustrated already. Joshua ignored her and continued to count his own consignment of chips and capacitors. They were individually packed in their own antistatic wraps. He didn't want to think what they were being used for. Visiting the data labs was one thing, but when you needed to go to the top floor for a meeting... He lost count and cursed under his breath.

Concentrating on getting the correct inventory he had completely forgotten that Rebecca was also in the room. He only noticed when she dropped a box of mobile phones that had been put aside for 'spares and repairs'. She swore loudly and hopped around for a few seconds, evidently it had landed on her foot. He saw her turn on one of the phones, its battered and cracked screen coming to life in an instant.

"Get over here..." she beckoned. He left his box of parts and walked to her. The room felt small although it was at least three times the size of their office. The metal racking and acoustic dampening that the boxes created made it seem claustrophobic. Rebecca was hurriedly finding the correct charging cable to plug into a nearby socket. Once she had located it she attached the phone and showed Joshua the screen.

Through the geometric maze of the cracked glass he could just about make out their intranet browser.

"I need to show you that folder. I wanted to use one of these phones as a proxy. Don't worry I know loads of people who've nicked them out of storage, nobody notices."

"I'm not sure this is a good idea..." Joshua was feeling odd again. The nausea in the pit of his stomach was not quite dread, but it could have been close. It was a semi-sickness, a clutching of muscles. It was nearing the feeling that he had tried to suppress for many years; the awful moment when he and the other children had witnessed the burnt wreck of the church - the sooty, incinerated remains of the crypt. The only computer, their only lifeline, melted into a sticky patch of sludge beneath the desecrated alabaster statue of the archangel Gabriel...

He brought himself back from the brink and swallowed.

"I really think we should finish getting the supplies as quickly as possible."

"Please let me show you, I won't actually go into the folder but I want to prove it exists at least." She turned the phone back towards her and navigated the browser. After a couple of difficult minutes her eyes lit up, triumphant. "There!" She let Joshua look at the screen again. He zoomed in on the storage for No Relevant Information.

Sorting the viewing panel by size he dragged the largest deleted file to the top.

"Well... you're right. That's the biggest amount of information left over from The Singularity that I've ever seen in one folder, in one location." He handed the phone back and she reviewed it.

"See, I told you - wait..." She squinted at the screen. "That can't be right." She stood next to Joshua to show him. "There, look at the access time. Nine this morning."

"Maybe someone was checking it, seeing as you brought it to their attention." She shook her head.

"This folder is bigger, I'm sure there was less in it yesterday... Is someone adding to this? What the fuck..." She was far too invested. Was she leaning against him? He stepped away, back to his shelf of inanimate, undemanding components.

"It's probably one of the new guys deleting stuff and it's just gone into that folder. He might have messed up the directories. You know what it's like searching all day, if you've got something open by accident and then..." He stopped talking. She was staring at him with a familiar aggrieved look.

"Really?" she said coolly.

"Yes?" he replied, not seeming convincing enough. She turned off the phone and then produced an alcohol-soaked cleaning wipe from a small packet in her pocket. She wiped the charger, the phone and the box to remove her fingerprints.

"It's not like I *want* to be suspicious. It's just that, well, five years doesn't seem that long in the grand scheme of things does it? Even World War Two lasted longer than the time it's taken for The Singularity to stay away. All sorts of things happen after a war has ended; all sorts of greedy people come out of the woodwork."

Joshua went back to the e-list on his phone and collected the last of the required parts. He put all the piles he'd made into separate padded envelopes and labelled them according to their destination. Then he put them into the bag. In silence, he waited for Rebecca to follow suit. Once they were both satisfied he unlocked the door from the inside. Rebecca walked past him to stand in the corridor with her own collection of envelopes under one arm. He turned off the light, closed the door and waited for the automatic lock to arm itself. After the three short beeps he nodded.

"Time to go then," he stated. She gazed at him, a smile playing around her lips.

"Okay partner."

*   *   *

The long trek to the data laboratories building was made in silence. The regular sound of their shoes on the carpet broke the tense atmosphere. Rebecca was playing with the lanyard round her neck. Joshua watched as her nimble fingers twisted the polyester ribbon into tangles and knots, then undid them just as skilfully. Once or twice she caught him looking and his face flushed with embarrassment, realising that she probably imagined he was staring at her breasts.

The lanyards had bothered him for a while. He had lain awake many nights in his grandfather's house wondering what it was that irked him so much. In the end he had come to the conclusion that it was the need to be visibly labelled. He contemplated that it could be an issue in his own mind from learning about the way the Jews were 'labelled' with stars pinned to their clothes. There was also something else.

Amid all this technology, why hadn't companies and governments kept the finger print scanners? The retinal scanners? The voice activated identity terminals? All of this equipment remained in situ after The Singularity left, yet it was unused. Lanyards were awkward, they clattered against office desks. When you leaned forward they got caught in clothing - sometimes even doors - if you were in a rush. When you forgot your lanyard, and therefore your means of identification, your wages would be docked or you would have to pay for a new plastic pass.

It seemed as if everyone who had flourished, and consequently been oppressed by the AI, was determined to make this new world as similar to the one they had forfeited decades before, faults and all. An over-bearing human need for nostalgia.

"I'll take this one." Rebecca had arrived outside a nondescript door to one of the labs. Joshua checked the number against the list on his phone

"Okay." He watched her knock. He watched the rat-like face of the laboratory assistant poke out of his hole and gobble up the new memory sticks. He saw the rectangular cavern of Stygian blackness that led to the airlock, the barrier between the real world and the clean room in the lab. Rebecca digitally signed off the delivery on her phone.

"Next?" she asked excitedly, and they started on the following leg of their journey.

Room after room, the same as always, hungry little men and women snatching at the supplies, engrossed with their duties and the promise of mediocre pay that they could spend on the ever-improving recreational activities. Soon there might even be a cinema in the town again. Joshua imagined that for a while it would show repeats of any films that hadn't been destroyed by the drones of the Sentient Neural Network.

His mother had been able to show him a few movies from her childhood before the Internet was fully disabled. They also had some DVDs stored in his grandfather's attic which he had watched over and over again. One Flew Over The Cuckoo's Nest, V For Vendetta, A Fist Full Of Dynamite, If..., and his favourite - 1984. Even after the DVD player was consigned to the scrap heap he read a tattered paperback copy of the book. Hiding his influences from his class mates at the weekend school that he was made to attend.

It was called a 'Compound School' by the townsfolk. Each educational building that was commandeered by The Singularity was patrolled along the perimeter by either assimilated humans or low-level guard drones. Not as advanced as the angels, these drones were merely there to be the eyes and ears of the Sentient Neural Network that formed the structure of the hive. They fed data back to the main hubs. They kept a check on who attended and who complied with class rules. He wondered how he had ever had the audacity to follow-up on the wealth of knowledge his classmates had accidentally uncovered. So many rotten books and ledgers, so much hidden power in those water-stained notepads under the floorboards... He had just wanted to be helpful.

He gripped the bundle of supplies through the fabric of the bag, his jaw tightening with stress. It was usual when he thought about his teenage years. So much work had gone into the small resistance faction, all for nothing. Burned to a crisp the moment they were on the brink of rebellion. His mother had said they were lucky; lucky not to be caught and exterminated. His grandfather had looked sad; watery-eyed and silent, remarking on the beautiful church that was also annihilated during in the night of destruction all those years ago.

One by one, he handed over his deliveries and greeted the recipients with a formal nod or a polite aside. Rebecca wanted to chat and ask details of the work they were doing, how they had found the new upgrades to the system. He wanted to be rapid and return to the office. He wanted to trawl through files and process mindless data in a less social environment.

"Just a few more to go!" his companion said cheerily. "All of these are on the top floor. Isn't this great?"

"Huh?" he replied dreamily.

"You know, going to the top. *Upstairs*. Getting the call." He raised an eyebrow.

"I'd rather stay under the radar if I'm honest." It was Rebecca's turn to shrug; mimicking his slack posture, jutting her bottom lip out.

"I don't want to get involved. It's all a bit too much effort if you ask me." She was putting on a deep male voice and a slightly bored tone, a caricature of him. Joshua found her humorous.

"Surely I'm not *that* bad?" he asked.

"*Surely* I'm not *that bad?*" she repeated in his exaggerated manner. Her eyes sparkled.

"Okay, okay, I promise to be more interested in your conversations about the company in the future," he said, a softness to his voice.

"Nice one! Well, you'll love what one of the techs back there told me." She was practically bubbling over with effervescent gossip. "They said the reason that we're doing two deliveries a week from the main storeroom is that there's been a massive influx of new data on the servers."

For a second Joshua's ears began to ring as his blood pressure rose. This was not good. More data, *new* data... there hadn't been any 'new' data since The Singularity went off-world. Rebecca was still babbling away, her little half-smiles and white teeth making the situation seem exciting. In his mind he was creating a ball of ice-cold fear that he pushed down.

"... So they're going for a meeting at the end of the week to create a new team to work on this until it stops coming in, or slows down a bit." Joshua didn't want to tell her that it wouldn't stop coming in. This was data deliberately being sent by someone.

Why had it started after five years of peace? God only knew... He smirked at his own turn of phrase. Religion was not going to save them this time. Rebecca playfully punched him on the arm.

"Don't laugh at me Josh! I'm serious!"

"I know you are. That's what I'm worried about."

"We could get moved onto the team together, maybe they'll even let me study that massive deleted folder - it could be the start of something huge." By this time they had walked to the end of one of the lab corridors and were faced with either several flights of sterile, plastic-coated stairs or a trip upwards in a goods lift. Joshua was fine with the stairs but Rebecca was already complaining about her feet aching.

"I didn't realise it would be such a hike!" she exclaimed. "I always forget the labs are so far away from the rest of the offices. Let's just take the lift... it's old but it's still working."

This was true. The lifts were regularly serviced, yet still they broke down at random and caused hundreds of pounds of expense for the government.

"We're not even carrying anything much, we haven't got a trolley," he argued. She displayed the remaining few bundles of supplies in her arms.

"Well what are these?" she said, ever the comedian, stooping, making them out to weigh a tonne.

For the sake of an easy life, and still trying to digest the information about the new data, he agreed to use the lift. They were going to the top floor and then walking along the corridor to the main offices where the CEOs and heads of department resided. The end of the top floor where the lift shaft was located boasted empty, partially decorated training rooms; wires hanging from the ceiling, desks still in their transport wrapping. It gave him the creeps every time he visited. It was as if they were expecting a sudden influx of workers to appear and populate the offices... This could have been the government's plan all along. Make them think the world had collapsed, then materialise workers from a secret facility.

They stepped into the lift at the same time, knocking elbows as they dodged the closing thick steel doors. It was industrial, probably older than he was. It had the feel of another life, another world. A world where trolleys filled with paper and pens could be wheeled from floor to floor. Stationery, mail, documents, all delivered by hand not by computer. Porters in company uniforms handing out important information. There were no mirrors or cameras inside the chamber. It was daubed with beige paint, scratched around the doorway, worn down to shiny silver metal then dirtied over time. Dilapidated.

They stood rather awkwardly as the doors came together. Josh hated the finality of the clunk and clank that happened as the lift locked into place on its cable. Neither of them pressed the button for floor twelve. Eventually they both leaned forward and their hands touched as they pressed the worn plastic together. It lit up a dull orange. They didn't move their fingers and Joshua had an unusual urge to clasp her hand to his chest. His heart was beating, the numbers counting up from three on the overhead LCD screen. She was looking at him, eyes wide and without thinking he dropped the empty stock bag he was holding. They embraced. Her remaining deliveries fell to the floor.

It was rough, passionate, both wondering if at any moment the lift would stop and they would be joined by a member of staff wanting to take the easy route. Joshua was burning with passion, he slipped his hand under her shirt and they clawed at each other, kissing frantically, fuelled by years of undisclosed sexual tension. Pressing their bodies as close as they could, gasping for breath with the shock of it all. Too soon the lift shunted into place and they almost lost their footing, flung sideways against a grimy wall. The orange light under the button for floor twelve was extinguished, as was their ardour.

They straightened their clothes and Rebecca picked up the crumpled bag from the floor, as well as her envelopes.

Taking care to stand as far apart as they could, they began to walk down the long corridor. Ahead of them the eerie, empty rooms at either side stood as a testament to hope. Hope that the economy would return to its glory days. Hope that soon it would be business as usual. Joshua spoke first. He tried to form a sentence but his voice broke and he laughed nervously, starting again and clearing his throat.

"Are... are you okay?" he asked, unsure. Rebecca smiled and tried to put several errant strands of hair back into her ponytail. She checked her shirt buttons as she walked, handing him the empty bag.

"Yes. Are you?"

"Yes!" he said, a little too quickly.

The corridor was getting wider. Some of the rooms had workmen in them putting wiring into white plastic conduits on the ceiling. They waved to the couple and Rebecca raised a friendly hand back. It came naturally to her, she was personable, something that he sorely envied. There were more windows here, light came through and Joshua realised that he had missed the sun for most of the day. LED strip lighting was no substitution for the real thing.

As they turned the first corner he hesitated. He checked his phone.

"Look, I, er, well, you're the only one with stuff left to deliver," he said clumsily. "Maybe I should head back now and make it seem less suspicious." Rebecca raised an eyebrow. "I mean, not that I don't want people to know, but I just think that -" She cut him short as he dug the hole deeper.

"Know what? Don't be a dickhead Josh. That bunch of cretins wouldn't know a romantic tryst if it slapped them in the face. I'll drop these things off and have a chat with the big guys on your behalf. You go back down and make me a cup of coffee..." she checked her phone for the time. "... in about thirty minutes, yeah?" He was delighted.

"Yeah. Yep. Yes, okay!"

She beamed too, her eyes warm with emotion. He felt something melting inside him, something that had been kept cold and aloof for too long. The shaft of sunlight from the window, the dust motes glistening as they fell, the clean, scented smell of her face powder... it seemed like a dream, a fantasy reserved for the sleepless nights and wasted weekends that he had been living for the last ten years. He waved as she walked away and all of a sudden felt foolish. This was ridiculous. A day ago she was nothing more than a colleague, now he was stumbling over his words and acting irrationally. He dug his fingernails into the palm of his hands as he headed for the nearest stairwell, finding a way out of the building as fast as he could. His phone buzzed and he picked up the message.

Rebecca: Can we do this properly?

His heart continued to race with excitement, without delay he replied.

My house for a meal?

He replaced his phone in his trouser pocket, determined not to look at it until he was back in his own office. However, it vibrated straight away. He resisted until he was in the stairwell, jogging down to the ground floor.

Rebecca: Tonight? I'll bring a board game.

He couldn't help but grin. This was unexpected, and for once it seemed that he was entitled to be optimistic. She already knew where he lived. It was far enough away from the main part of the town to allay her anxiety about being watched. He could show her the garden that was coming to life; she'd like that. The last of the winter frost had given way to snowdrops and early crocuses.

*   *   *

More than two hours passed and Rebecca had not returned to the office. Outside the leaden sky promised rain, and Joshua's co-workers were making the most of the free hot drinks in the kitchenette. Huddled around the kettle, whispering, they reminded him of children; overlooked, nervous, safer in a crowd. He pushed past them and made another cup of coffee. He set it down next to the cold one that had been left on the conspicuously empty desk. Making his way back to his own seat under the accusatory gaze of his associates his mettle hardened.

No-one here was 'bad' per se; they had their own demons to deal with. Everyone bore baggage of The Singularity in invisible ways. It could be the constant pen-tapper, the lip biter, the day-dreamer, the moral 'saint'. These anxious young adults lived in a stress-inducing tug of war between fear of the machines returning and daring to hope that the world was fixing itself for their prolonged future.

Joshua, on the other hand, was pessimistic from the off. He had used up all of his optimism before his twentieth birthday, and now he wanted to survive long enough to... he wondered, not for the first time, what he was living for? No parents, no grandparents. No close family. He leaned back on his chair and looked at the mass of information on his computer screen.

Maybe he was living so that he could help untangle the mess that had been left behind. He imagined that as a team their sorting, filing and deleting of information had an international impact on the generation below him; providing insight into useful technology, maybe even cures for diseases that had once again reared their ugly heads. He smiled to himself. Maybe it wasn't so bad. He had a dinner date organised with someone he could tolerate, and he was being a useful member of society.

His colleagues started to pack their belongings away. Pens and e-cigarettes were dutifully slotted into bags, mobile phones were checked and then turned off for the long trudge home. Steven exchanged some pleasantries with Joshua, explaining how he was hoping to go fishing at the weekend with his son. Joshua smiled politely. Younger than him, Steven had a ten year old son and two young daughters. He was living the new era procreation propaganda to a T.

Once everyone had left the office Joshua cleared away the forlorn-looking untouched cups of coffee and glanced nervously at Rebecca's handbag, still stuffed unceremoniously under her desk, bunched up against the back wall. Should he move it? He checked his phone. Still no message. He wondered why he was allowing himself to get concerned. This would never have happened a day ago, even this morning. He wouldn't have cared about some insignificant handbag, he was reading too much into things as usual. It was that damned kiss... those stupid, humorous asides... his nagging conscience. Just to appease his growing anxiety, he decided to send her a message.

Leaving work now. See you later.

It was formal enough, but also reminded her that they had made plans. He wondered if she had forgotten in all the excitement of being invited to the top floor offices. The message in reply was almost instantaneous.

Rebecca: Of course.

This must be what it felt like to be infatuated with someone. To be wanted. He could not recall a time when he had been appreciated for who he was, simply as a person. It was all very well being applauded for your technical prowess, for your usefulness, but quite another thing to know that someone wanted to choose to spend time with you... just because they were interested in 'you'. He thought of all the times he had chosen to be with his mother: watching a film, discussing a theory over a mug of weak tea. He had wanted to hear her, be there for her.

He wondered if it was the primeval fear of losing her, his only parent, that had urged him to stick around. Did he remember any of her ideals now? No. He remembered her face, her voice - to a degree - but her exact political bias and morality was alien to him. Could the same be said of his interactions with the rest of the people still present in his life?

*   *   *

Walking through the town as night fell, Joshua could have been anywhere. New York, Toronto, Tokyo, they were all in a similar state of regeneration. He pondered the fact that many of the 'third world' countries, and indeed their 'fourth world' aboriginal colonies, were not so affected by the reign of the machines as the major economic powers. He imagined they had less to lose; less material obsession, more of an enduring survival mode.

If you spent all day collecting fire wood and food in a remote rainforest, you probably wouldn't care if that thing overhead was a helicopter with a fascinated TV crew on board, or an angelic guard sent to monitor you. Both were irrelevant and had no impact on your daily routine.

He caught himself boarding one of the electric shuttle buses. It was all but empty as usual. When he pressed his wallet to the scanner, the driver waved him on without even checking that his fare had registered. The buses were hard, cold and smelled of newly formed plastic. He had heard some of the older people refer to it as a pervading 'new car' fragrance that never went away. Some people felt travel-sick, after so many years of not using vehicles. Joshua felt trapped, and he rarely used them for such a short distance. Today he had wanted to get home as swiftly as he could.

The bus seats were moulded from one large sheet of blue plastic with chartreuse rubber pads, indicating that they seated three people on each side of the aisle. Easily cleaned and easily repaired. The harsh white lights ran in rows along the full length of the single deck ceiling. They illuminated every gaunt, resolute face of his travelling companions. The bus passed by stops and shelters, untenanted, even by the ubiquitous youths who seemed to lurk on every street corner. Maybe it was too bitter for them tonight.

He looked down at his clothes: his trousers, his coat, his shoes, his messenger bag. How did he appear to the other commuters? They were haggard and some were unshaven. He had maintained that good personal hygiene hid a wealth of issues, both mental and physical. Did any of them know him? Did they know he had inherited such a nice house on one of the 'good' streets? Did they envy his garden and legacy left by his grandfather when times had been tough?

He had contacts in many sectors of local retail, most of them in procurement departments. Not that he'd ever called on them. He doubted he ever would now that the economy was on the up. He didn't need to be reminded of the things he had done to secure a tin of meat or a pack of pills for his family. He'd rather remain unapproachable. Better to be considered a snob than a scrounger.

Did Rebecca see him as a 'catch', a man with money after The Singularity, somewhat of a middle-class bachelor? Her parents had run the post office for a time; they had even franchised the cinema. She had her own flat, they had their own terraced house near the town centre; all good assets. Maybe she wanted more. Could it be that she wanted a family and security? To be one of those young mothers who slouched on the main road with pushchairs and sour mouths. Standing in gaggles like depressed avian hoards, squawking about who shagged who. Who stole someone's Giro slip…

"It's your stop mate." The bus driver had craned his neck around and was staring at Joshua. He wasn't angry, just exhausted. "Come on son. I haven't got all day."

Joshua apologised and alighted at the usual stop, two roads away from his house. With the sun well below the horizon it exposed the lack of street lights and the blackout curtains in most windows. He had forgotten for a while that people had gone to war in the old-fashioned way. He had learned about the traditional art of war from his grandfather, from some books with sepia photographs. Their conversations were tactical and filled with facts, unlike those with his mother who fought on an emotional level. He learned about his great grandfather and how he had fought in both the first and second world wars as a private. He learned about the people who had to try and continue living in war-torn countries. Blackout curtains, keep hidden, don't trust a soul; these were all well and good when your aggressor was human.

In the 'war' against the AI, the all-knowing neural network was always one step ahead. It had maps, census results, real-time mobile information and wireless connections with which to gather intelligence. People blocking up their windows with cardboard and thick curtains was more for their own psyche than to be hidden from the sinister, constant gaze of the machine-led soldiers.

Chinks of warm light escaped into the gloom forming bright geometric patterns, seemingly coming out of nowhere. Front gardens littered with broken appliances were at last invisible, tidy under the veil of night. It was beautiful in its own way, but also sad. His feet carried him the short distance home and he stood back to survey his property. Normal. Identical to his neighbours on either side. A paved driveway covered in weeds and debris. The remains of his grandfather's silver Volvo, rusting in the same spot, flat tyres and sunken, pock-marked exterior. The house windows needed to be cleaned. They were visibly streaked with dirty rain water. No reflection. He looked back to the car and guessed that even when the machines came to reclaim metal scrap it was already beyond use.

The overgrown kerbside garden was exactly that. He'd had no time to tend the front of the house since he started work at the office. In the past he would have taken out the hoe, the edging tool and made a start on the weeds and tufts of grass. Somewhere, beneath the strip of dirt that had been covered by unwanted plants, there were bulbs and tubers waiting to burst through, but the chickweed and creeping buttercup held them at bay.

He barely had time to tinker around in the back yard with some of the flower pots. He always kept the area tidy. He even weeded the empty spaces so that the fertile brown earth could show through. He never got further than planning what he wanted to plant. He had wanted peas this year, easy to grow and not much maintenance. He had prepared a few huge planters at the side of the house. Now it all looked like a mini, barren demolition site. With a couple of small model soldiers he could recreate the Somme.

He hoped that Rebecca would find it quaint, endearing. He hoped that she would walk up the back path and use the side door to the house, step into the kitchen and feel like she could relax… His mind wandered as he imagined how the evening would play out. He was lost in his own thoughts when he realised that somebody was speaking to him. It was Philip. He was holding a bunch of fresh flowers tied with a purple ribbon, their colours muted by the twilight.

"You okay mate?" he shouted, from much too far away. Joshua raised his hand.

"Fine thanks." He tried to avoid the man at all costs. It brought back too many memories. He was walking quite forcefully towards Joshua, the unseasonal flowers bouncing in their vibrant bouquet.

Philip had put on weight. Some of his tattoos were faded and his once rugged 'lumber-jack' look had turned into more of an 'over-the-hill biker having a generic middle-aged crisis'. He was panting heavily and Joshua smelled alcohol on his breath.

"You're home late," he said jovially. "Hard day at the office, eh?" He was invading Joshua's personal space, sweat and stale beer overpowering his cologne.

"I guess so. It's not as interesting as people think, sifting through data." Philip smiled and emitted a kind of snort-chuckle.

"You've got your mother's dry wit!" There was an awkward silence. "You've been up there recently?" he asked.

Joshua knew he meant the cemetery. It always peeved him the way that this man, this creature, had the gall to visit his mother's grave. Most of the reason she went downhill so fast was that tawdry affair. Granted Philip had gone on to marry *that woman*, but at what price?

"Yes, I go up a few times a week actually. Just to check on... the family." Philip wasn't picking up on the acetous atmosphere. He never did. Even when Joshua was learning how to shoot a rifle with him up in the back woods, he would never sense when to shut up and move on from a subject.

"I'm just off myself actually, yeah, anniversary and all that. Sad, sad times."

"Anniversary of what?" asked Joshua on impulse.

"The day I met your mum. It's always the same every year. Jan hates it. I can't help it. She was the love of my life y'know..." He looked as if he was going to cry. Joshua wasn't prepared for this emotional onslaught and wished that the man would go on his way. "Jan always says we're only together because she's dead. If your mum was here... I'd be..." He loosely waved the bunch of flowers. A salmon coloured rose head fell to the ground.

"That's all done now though. You can't change the past," Joshua mumbled. A couple of decrepit cars rattled past, their headlights catching the tears on Philip's grizzled face. He looked old. He probably *was* old. He had been older than his mum when they met all those years ago.

"Wise words son. Doesn't help the old -" he patted his chest above his heart, "ticker though does it?" Joshua gritted his teeth.

"I wouldn't know."

They stood facing each other. The first specks of rain fell, creating a blanket of fine silver droplets on their clothes.

"You're not seeing anyone yet?" The 'yet' hung in the night air. This man could have been his father figure. He could have grown up with a stable representation of a patriarchy. Instead he had been saddled with a disinterested grandfather and a volatile mother.

"Maybe something on the horizon, but I'm not sure," he answered cautiously. Philip took the bull by the horns and wiped an arthritic hand across, his face.

"That's the spirit! Good for the soul. A nice woman and everything that goes along with that." He stepped closer, nudging Joshua in the ribs. "Soon have that empty house filled with the pitter-patter of tiny feet. Our Sarah's on her fourth now, can you believe it?"

Joshua could believe it. 'His Sarah' was a woman that spent most of her time trying to repopulate the South of England single-handedly.

"Good news then; I hope it's healthy," he replied with as much sincerity as he could. Philip looked at the flowers, and then up at Joshua; his happy-go-lucky expression dampened slightly, and not just from the drizzle.

"Me and your mum... we... well, did she ever tell you?" Joshua closed his eyes. Not this again. Maybe he had been drinking more than his upright demeanour was letting on. "Would've been a teenager now... a little brother or sister for you... I always wonder what -" Joshua cut him off.

"I need to make a phone call. Sorry." He didn't sound sorry, and Philip didn't seem to care. He was wallowing in his own sentimentality.

"Right-o lad, I'll be off up the road then. Bit of a walk for me, best leave Jan to get over her jealousy - silly old mare. We really should get together soon for a proper catch up. Jan makes a mean chilli con carne. It would be good if you could bring us some of your famous Scotch Bonnets." Joshua ignored him and walked towards the house, fumbling for his keys and hoping that Philip would meet a sticky end on the way to the cemetery. He wondered what women saw in him. Even when he was younger he was a hulk of a man; beer-belly, gruff, coarse with his humour. Joshua supposed it was the fact that he got things done. He had once been in the army, fought in a couple of conflicts. He was handy with his DIY skills. Those kinds of things were useful when all the trouble started.

Entering the dark house he noticed a smell of damp. Not the terrible damp that could eat away floorboards and stain walls, but an absence of air movement. He switched on the kitchen light. The room was pristine. It was something he had wanted to do after his grandfather died. They had always lived in such turmoil, saving scraps of material, paper, wood. All these essential things would be kept in little piles around the house.

Joshua remembered when he made a den under the stairs. The space was surprisingly big, and he stuck drawings he'd made onto the 'ceiling' with pins. A few years after that, they were removed and used to write down lists for customers who needed special orders from the allotment. Without a thought for their worth, he and his grandfather had torn them into quarters and written on the blank sides... This house was a museum of memories. It was a tomb. He hoped that having dinner with Rebecca would erase at least some of the ghosts that clung to him.

*   *   *

After changing out of his work clothes and into a more relaxed outfit, he ran a damp cloth across all the kitchen and living room surfaces. Dust collected in grey lines on the yellow fabric, and he was dismayed to see milky streaks remaining along the mantelpiece. He lifted all the ornaments off and cleaned it properly. Checking his phone he saw that it was already half past seven. What time had they arranged? He looked at the messages. It said 'tonight'. When was tonight? Was that now? Was that ten o'clock? It couldn't be too late as they needed to eat a meal and they were both working the next day. Did she think she was staying over? Had she changed her mind?

He wrung the duster between his hands, twisting it, mimicking the way his stomach felt; in knots. If this was the first flutter of butterflies then the romantics could keep them. He felt ill and anxious. After breathing calmly for a few moments he decided to concentrate on cooking. He took a pizza out of the freezer and set it next to the oven. Then he sought out a packet of dry pasta twirls. He wondered if the meagre crop of tomatoes in the greenhouse were ready to pick yet, he could use them in the sauce... All of this was a good distraction. He needed to be doing something physical, something that took his mind off the 'date'.

Another hour passed. No message. No update. No social media profile activity. He decided to cook some of the food and eat his own meal to settle his aching stomach. In the meantime he cleaned the bathroom and put out a fresh hand towel from the airing cupboard. The house was silent.

Another hour passed. He had eaten his pasta and pizza at the kitchen table, his phone face down so he could ignore the temptation to check it every five minutes. He decided to find some music to put on and went to the living room to look through the small selection of CDs that had belonged to his family. He recognised the names, he remembered a few of the songs, but he wasn't sure which one would set the mood. In the end he chose a compilation of Motown music that had been free with a Sunday newspaper aeons ago. He eased it carefully out of the cardboard sleeve and sat for a while on the sagging sofa, letting the excited drum beats and singing wash over him. The people sounded happy...

Another hour passed. Ten thirty. It was too late. The

rain was teeming down outside, it bounced off the greenhouse roof. He could hear it over the music and it made him angry. Was this some kind of joke to her? Had she regretted their moment of passion? He felt every muscle in his face strain with anger. So this was what it felt like to be scorned. He cursed himself for being so erratic over the last few days. He should never have accepted the invitation to visit her flat and discuss that stupid folder full of insignificant, *irrelevant* deleted data!

He was in the kitchen, pacing up and down. Acrimonious. Blaming himself. Blaming her... As he walked past the sink he grabbed a worn ceramic mug and threw it to the floor. It shattered with a pleasing explosion. He picked up a small plate, flinging it downwards to the same fate as the rest of the crockery. In fact he was so heated that he threw the whole drainer full of drying cups, plates and cutlery onto the floor with an almighty smash. At the same time it hit the floor the music stopped in the living room, and there was another noise. Someone was knocking on the back door.

His feet turned to lead. He froze. Rebecca. She was just late! He must have sounded like a maniac! Maybe she had tried the front door and got no response because of the music, besides everyone used the back door at the side, she might not have realised. The thoughts whirled around his head until he was forced to hold onto the work top.

The knocking continued, along with a gruff voice. "Hello? Hello? Are you alright in there?" This wasn't the voice of a young woman, it was the voice of Philip. "Josh – answer me right now or I'm coming in!" Joshua felt embarrassed and upset all at the same time. He wished the kitchen floor would open up into a chasm, consuming him and the clutter. He steadied himself.

"Yeah, yes... I'm actually okay thanks, just knocked a few things off the side..." He didn't sound sure.

"I don't want to be rude son, but, I'm coming in to check..." Of course he was, thought Joshua; his palms clammy from anxiety. He started to clear up the mess by hand, bending down and picking up the bigger shards of china.

Philip pushed the door open, he was drenched. His coat and trousers were sodden, the gale raging behind him had picked up to biblical strength. He looked down at Joshua and the devastation. Then he looked at the single clean plate and empty wine glass on the table.

"I saw the light on in the living room, I didn't want to interrupt anything, it's just -" He shut the door behind him. Joshua realised that this was probably the first time in a decade that the man had set foot inside the house. They had spoken outside many times, even shared some produce from the back garden, but he hadn't been inside since the...

"Am I interrupting something?" It was the first time Joshua had seen him act with any form of etiquette.

"No, it's only me," he muttered, still on his knees.

Philip sat down at the kitchen table. He didn't appear to want to help. He seemed defeated, deflated. Through tight lips, Joshua asked him what was wrong. He sighed over-dramatically, as he was prone to do.

"I've done it. I've really done it this time." Joshua stopped tidying and put the shards already in his hand into the bin. They were cold, jagged and far beyond mending.

"Done what?" he asked unemotionally. Philip sighed again and looked around the kitchen. It was the same as it had always been. The papers on the cork notice board were a little more discoloured, ragged around the edges, some of the fridge magnets had failed the test of time, but essentially it was the same room.

"I told Jan it's over. I had to tell her the truth. I couldn't do it anymore. I couldn't keep up this stupid pretence." Joshua leaned against the worktop, fearing that if he sat at the table Phil would take that as an indication to keep talking. He seemed even more inebriated than before. "I went to see your mum, didn't I? Jan wouldn't let up; all this bad-mouthing, all this slander against a poor dead woman who can't defend herself." He sounded woeful, genuine. But Joshua had had his share of psychological bombardment already. This sad fat man at his table was an intrusion. He was picking at damaged flesh that had barely scabbed over. "... I shouted at her, I told her I never loved her and that if Annie was still alive today I'd be living here with you lot, like a real family."

Joshua winced at his mum being called Annie. He

remembered how Philip had insisted on calling her 'my little Annie'. The man was in tears now, laying his head in his hands. Joshua reached for the old garden broom that was in the corner of the kitchen by the fridge.

"It's just an argument. You'll get over it soon enough," he said plainly. Philip looked up at him with bloodshot eyes, saliva in his grey beard and moustache.

"It – It was a big row! Not just an argument. I'm surprised you didn't hear it – she's chucked me out for good... can't stay with our Sarah or our Melanie... they took her side, they always do, they never knew your mum..." He sniffed wetly. "I was hoping I could..." He looked, beseechingly, at Joshua who continued sweeping.

"I'm expecting company," he responded, without looking at the man.

Philip stood up, infuriated now, all hint of social courtesy gone.

"Well screw you Josh! I thought us guys would stick together! I thought you'd at least let me have one of the bedrooms, I'd pay rent - I've got a job you know!" He stood up, gesticulating, face bright red. "She's your mum!"

"Was. She *was* my mother," corrected Joshua.

"And don't I know it! Every day I see you walk past the house, every day I remember that you told me I'd killed her! She wasn't a saint, but I fucking loved her!" He threw the wooden chair backwards and it collided with the wall. "You think you're so much better than us, you think you're so much smarter with your cushy job in the civil service, working with all them government officials! You wait and see, they'll be after you soon enough when they know the truth - and then where will this -" he gestured at the room, the house - "get you?" Joshua walked to the back door and opened it. Rain blew into the kitchen and began to douse his arm, spattering the sleeve of his sweatshirt.

"I think you should leave."

*　　　*　　　*

The morning came, and with it a sense of detachment. Daylight crept through the master bedroom, poking its way through the thin curtains and bringing soft breezes through the gaps in the window casement. Joshua turned over in the large double bed. He wrapped the duvet around him like a cocoon. Any moment now his phone alarm would burst into shrill song, his head was aching and his eyes were sore.

The duvet smelled comforting. He could never have brought a woman back here. What was he thinking? This was his sanctuary. The kitchen had been tainted by Philip, but up here in the lofty heights he still had his dignity and solace. Up here he was out of reach of the everyday life where people hurt each other, where people robbed and stabbed and fought their way through existence. He could lay in bed and shut out the responsibilities that had been placed on him.

His phone alarm sprang into life and he silenced it. He had exactly fifteen minutes before he needed to get up and take a shower. Then sixty minutes to get dressed and eat breakfast. Then forty-five minutes to get to work on foot. Why had he even tried to complicate things by following his heart? What did his heart know anyway? He liked Rebecca but she was eccentric and daring. She wanted to poke at the beast and then wondered why it bit back... he would do his best to act as if everything was normal again.

No accepting of invitations, no extra cups of coffee, no doughnuts. No talking, no eye contact, the same as before. Safe, quiet, orderly. He closed his eyes. For all his resolutions he couldn't silence the tightness, the pain in his chest. He had known her for so many years. They were holders of a catastrophic secret. They had an unspoken trust, albeit from different angles.

His mind strayed back to those days in the Compound School. Rebecca and her brothers sitting motionless; all of them mute as the assimilated human teacher dictated and instructed about circuit boards, solder and the great opportunities that automation would bring to the world. So much rhetoric and hardly any facts... then they had found the books, the knowledge... then they had set up the network with the other rebels, fearful that one of the younger children would expose their clandestine project.

She had always been there in the background. Watching, advising. When she left to work at an AI-run facility in the city Joshua couldn't say that he felt her absence, yet he had felt an impulse to shake her hand and wish her well. When they had met again randomly in the data labs at their current employment he had been pleasantly surprised. She was the one person that had always tried to talk to him, or *at* him, every day; even when he gave no answer or tried to distance himself. Her snub last night had been more painful than he cared to admit.

*   *   *

The walk to work was accompanied by unexpected sunlight. After last night's storm, scraps of clouds, torn from their host, hurried across the sky. He looked up at that powder-blue expanse and recalled the years when, shining back like daytime stars, the hordes of angels would be hovering. Flying so high that ordinarily they were invisible, but on sunny days their white exoskeletons would be belied by their reflective quality. Now all that resided on high were military planes and the occasional pigeon.

He felt sombre. It was the perfect word to describe his mood. No matter how hard he tried he couldn't muster even a hint of a smile. His mouth felt as if it was permanently locked in a downward pose. Other workers greeted him, tried to pass the time of day, offered him raffle tickets for on-going charity fund-raisers. All he could do was make eye contact and stop the flood of sadness that was being held back by a few small facial muscles. His eyelid twitched.

He pushed his way through the sea of lab coats and suits; up the stairs, through the maze of corridors and side rooms, eventually ending up at his office with just two minutes to spare. He chastised himself for dawdling. Usually he arrived ten minutes early, even on foot. People were plugging headphones in, putting in their contact lenses, making tea and coffee. There was a moderate level of commotion. The room felt full.

Joshua went to the single window and pulled the blind up so that that the spring sun could penetrate as far as his desk. On his way past Rebecca's seat he noticed the coffee cup rings from yesterday were still marking the surface. He rubbed them with the cuff of his shirt but they didn't budge. He moved her chair out of the way to get into a better position to tackle the stains, and the wheels caught on something. Bending down, he saw that it was the strap of Rebecca's handbag.

He froze.

The bag was in exactly the same spot he had left it in the night before. He saw the same pattern of creases where it had been pushed against the wall, one of the handles had looped over her chunky key-chain accessories tied to the zip. He knew the bag hadn't been moved. She would also never have let a coffee stain sit there overnight; her sparkling white kitchen was a testament to that.

So as not to draw attention to the matter, he used his left hand to unhook the strap from the wheel and scoot the bag along, as close as he could, to his own desk. Then, very cautiously, while still on his knees, he took a USB flash drive out of his trouser pocket and dropped it on the floor. Standing up, he patted himself down and made an exasperated face, a show for any of his co-workers who happened to catch his eye. He sat at his desk and turned on his terminal.

While it was loading up he feigned spotting his flash drive by Rebecca's chair, and dashed across to collect it. Steve called over to him;

"Better be careful, those are hot property. They're not giving us any more until next quarter." Joshua feigned a smile.

"Oh yeah? Budget cuts already, we're only in year two of this campaign." Steve raised his mug of tea.

"Here's to the new world economy, civil servants are always the first to suffer!" Joshua smiled again and sat back in his seat. The tips of his shoes were touching Rebecca's bag. His heart was hammering against his ribcage.

A familiar feeling was coursing through his veins, this wasn't despair or depression. This was undiluted fury. This was injustice. He felt the palms of his hands begin to heat up, blood rushing to his head as he tried to put the pieces together. Before jumping any further to conclusions he decided to message her one more time. Trying not to raise suspicion he waited until she was fifteen minutes 'late' for work.

Hi, is everything alright? Are you running late?

Unlike yesterday there was no response. He played around with the phone for a while, scrolled through the paltry selection of intranet updates, and decided to visit Rebecca's profile. He studied her photo. She was holding a large ginger cat, looking away from the camera. He could make out her parents in the blurred background. He checked her newsfeed. No activity since they had parted ways the day before.

He wanted to make a plan of action. He had to do this away from technology; his survival mode kicked in. The company were obviously monitoring everything the employees did and said. They must have realised she had changed the delivery rota, they must have worked out she had used a phone from the storeroom to access the deleted folder.

After a few minutes he came up with a feasible idea. He would advise his manager via email that he needed to go home as he was feeling unwell. He would covertly stuff Rebecca's bag into his own, and take it with him. Once he was at home and away from the company he would use some cracked software on one of his laptops to hack in through the back door of their system and look at the deleted folder for himself.

When he knew what he was dealing with, he could think about Rebecca's safety and go to the authorities with proof of her abduction. To add weight to his plan he made several trips to the employee toilets, with sound effects, and after completing a few small tasks online he sat for a while holding his stomach, looking at the floor. An hour and a half later he sent a brusque email to his manager and copied in the human resources department. It made him even more riled that the standard reply was simply 'if you must'. He had met his manager once, a pat on the shoulder and a 'welcome to the department meeting' was all he received.

Slowly he bent down and thrust Rebecca's bag into his own. It was made quite difficult by the fact that she had a lunch box and a mini umbrella in there. He managed to jam it in by taking out his water bottle, stashing it under his desk. He straightened up and put on his coat. A few of his fellow workers raised their eyebrows and he gestured apologetically. Nobody made a move to say good bye. He hoped it was because they didn't want to catch his sickness, not because he was a condemned man.

*   *   *

Walking as calmly as he could he exited the building. He was waiting for the next bus, occasionally clutching his abdomen and looking at his phone. Somewhere above him on the top floor he was sure he was being monitored. Having rarely taken a sick day, he prayed that his employers would not see the correlation between this absence and the sudden 'disappearance' of his colleague.

How could a trusted government-funded company do this to someone? After the atrocities faced by humanity - subjugated by the machines, spied on and pillaged by an uncaring overlord - he wished that they had learned their lesson. He was feeling that old world-weary way again. The way he felt when he laid the cables and wires in the crypt. The way he felt when he learned how to monitor the network traffic on the old lines. The way he felt when he helped to organise the other teenagers into a crew. It was as if he was walking uphill, endlessly heading for a peak that was out of reach.

The shuttle bus eventually turned up in all its silent, electric glory. The sun continued to shine. People in the town went about their business; shopping on the high street, chatting to old friends. He watched them through the flexi-glass window and envied their ignorance. Without being reminded, he got off at his stop. Puddles from the storm had not yet evaporated. They pooled on the cracked tarmac like broken mirrors, only reflecting part of their surroundings and never telling the full story. He kicked a couple as he walked past, the water spraying out catching the light, for just a second, in a rainbow arc.

Passing by Philip's house he looked through the living room window. It was unobscured. Their whole front garden had been tarmacked years ago so that they could fit as many vehicles as possible on at one time. Now it was empty. He could see the television in the corner of the room, it was turned off. They had a similar set-up with a sofa and arm chairs as he did. Nobody was in the living room, but above that he caught a movement in the master bedroom window. Philip's wife Jan was walking back and forth on her mobile phone. She looked down and met Joshua's eye. For a moment she paused and they held each other's attention, then she walked away, out of sight.

He went inside as quickly as he could, locking the back door behind him. Before finding his laptop and other devices, he decided to go through Rebecca's bag for a clue, anything that could explain why she had been taken. He took out the lunch box, the umbrella, feminine items, a purse with her ID and a few bank cards, and then in the lining he felt the rectangular outline of a mobile phone. He located a secret zipped internal pouch between the lining and the outer bag. The phone was active and had lots of message icons on the front screen. The mobile data symbol was flashing and instinctively Joshua worried that the phone was being tracked. He was surprised to find that there was no pin code to unlock, and no fingerprint scan either.

Upon further inspection it wasn't an 'active' phone; it was being used as a storage device. The 'messages' he could see on the screen were notes, presumably typed by Rebecca. He read some of them.

"554267 GB 12:46" and another read *"557884 GB 13:20"*.

There were photographs of company computer screens with more information on them, photographs of broken phone screens. A whole wealth of research, but for what?
"Oh no..." he whispered. The words fell out of his mouth.

Something was very wrong. She had uncovered something that was supposed to remain buried.

He got together his equipment, and then started looking through the screen shots on the secret phone for the name of the specific folder she had shown him. He wished he'd paid more attention in the storeroom when she accessed it. After a lot of false starts, he found the file he was looking for and used his secondary laptop to create a virtual machine with which he could break into his employer's system.

* * *

This all took longer than he had anticipated. It wasn't until late afternoon that he was able to locate the original deleted file in the mass of junk and obsolete reports that had ended up on the digital scrap heap. At first he wasn't sure it was the right folder. The extension was slightly different and it looked as if it had been deleted into the trash folder that day, rather than a couple of days before. It was also larger than the most recent notes on Rebecca's phone had indicated.

This was one of the most frightening aspects of the whole ordeal. If something was being continually deleted as it grew in size, that meant that an 'active' folder was being followed... and being added to. If the folder was filled with information relating to every person on Earth, the only things that would need to be updated were births, deaths, and crimes. The New World Order was advanced, but they weren't *that* advanced; which left only one option. The Singularity had never truly left.

Outside the kitchen window the light was fading into dusk. He was very aware of being left visually exposed. Philip, or an equally interfering neighbour, could easily see in and photograph his laptop screen. He checked that the back door was still locked and he closed the curtains. This did nothing to assuage his uneasiness. Eventually he decided that the only safe space to work was from his bedroom where he could hide himself away and be certain that nobody was spying on him.

It was a laborious task to dismantle the multiple laptops and power cables, but after a few trips he had the set-up replicated on his bedside table. The bedroom curtains were pulled tight and held in place with a broken plastic hair clip. He had seen it under the bed in the spare room. It had once belonged to his mother.

He remembered her hastily scrunching her hair up into some sort of bun before forcing the teeth of the clip into the tangle, cursing as the cheap plastic scraped her scalp... it was odd that he always referred to it as the spare room. He could say Mum's old room, the back room... All the rooms bar his own were spare. Who would he be able to share them with anyway? He very much doubted he'd be seeing Rebecca again. He ground his teeth together, feeling them catch on each other.

Maybe he was sick. Sick in the head. He could be losing it like his mother. He could be a powder keg of frustration and fear; despair and anger welling up until he went completely cuckoo. He remembered the way she used to lay in the bed staring at the ceiling, especially near the end. She would sing to herself quietly, broken refrains of long-forgotten pop songs; the only reference she had for normality in such an alien world created by The Singularity.

His grandfather had tried his best to accept the changes; starting a food bank for the neighbourhood, learning about cultivation and nutrients, petitioning for use of the council allotments for community food production. He had taken up the mantle of 'provider' for a while. Joshua missed the summer days spent tending to the crops. It was a welcome relief from the strain of setting up the illegal technology network. After hours of undercover trips to the church or to a supporter's house, he could run his hands through feathery carrot tops, and pick caterpillars off swelling cabbages. Nature went on despite the machines and their regime. You couldn't tell a weed not to grow between the cracks in the concrete.

Well, maybe you could.

You could nuke the entire planet, lay waste to all life forms except your own.

Where would that leave you? Master of nothing. King of a dead, desolate world.

He turned his attention back to the task at hand. The curtains were closed, his virtual machines and proxies had been reinstated, and in front of him was the digital folder that had caused all of this trauma. Did his work mates know that Rebecca was missing yet? Did they know that he was lying about his illness? Did they realise he had fallen in love? If they joined the dots and connected her disappearance with yesterday's delivery schedule change, he could be in deep, deep trouble. All it took was one suggestion from a 'concerned' colleague and he would be done for.

The folder looked innocent enough. There was nothing different in its appearance to that of any other extracted information that had been passed to them from the data labs. Something was niggling at him, it was such a big folder. Things like this always went through a process of checks and inspections before being deleted. Rebecca would have innocently assumed that one of the interns had made a mistake, but in reality it was difficult to make a 'mistake' of that magnitude. The government were dealing with sensitive data, important data. Everything being transferred onto the Central Hub for the world to access had to be screened and deemed relevant. Essentially they were cleansing the history of the reign of The Singularity.

He had tried to stay impartial, yet he found himself getting drawn back into his former role of insurgent. Did the general population know that there was this over-riding filter veiling the titbits of knowledge that they were fed? Probably not, they were just as blinkered as ever. Their information was being filtered and distilled through stages until the last degree; mainstream media, turned it into a palatable 'story'. Whether they believed it or not was another matter.

He opened the system information that stated where and when the folder had been deleted, a kind of digital paper trail that every item had. It was a unique fingerprint that could not easily be tampered with and it allowed the technicians to discern any false data being deleted or added to the infrastructure before they entered it onto the Central Hub. The trail was long, full of locations, dates, times. He scrolled through for what seemed like minutes. Eventually he ended up at the source and blinked.

The location was not one of the server addresses that he recognised. It seemed legitimate, but he had been working for the department for long enough to know all the server ID addresses, and this was definitely not one he'd encountered before. Cautiously Joshua used the virtual machine he was on to find the list of all viable servers that the AI had 'gifted' to humanity before going off-world. He even checked the 'dead' machines, full of nothing but partially-rendered dream data. Ghosts, phantoms that the network had used to store all of its developmental statistics as it grew into the behemoth of The Singularity. And no, this particular server was not included in that list either.

Out of curiosity, he scanned the whole infrastructure for any record of the server at all, even using a small part of the ID. No matches. He went back to the offending folder to look for more clues. The deletion date and the employee that carried out the action could be of help... He was, again, confronted with a long string of text which he deciphered quickly.

It showed the deletion date as a year ago. There was no record of the employee who deemed the file to contain No Relevant Information. He wondered if the employee had since left the company and there had been some administration error that meant the ID was also terminated. If the AI was still monitoring the population, anything could be possible. In the beginning it had created a believable avatar and dominated media platforms taking over national elections. By the time it went off-world it was capable of everything. Building a fake employee ID would be child's play.

As he sat musing over these inconsistencies, he was thrown out of the folder. His screen went blank momentarily and he was forced back to the virtual machine main page on his laptop. As a matter of course he checked that all of his devices had power and were working correctly. He checked the error log – nothing. Assuming it was a security update from the company he went through the stages of hacking the system again. It was tedious. Finally he was back at the folder.

Except that it wasn't the same as before.

It had grown in size. He opened it up and, rather than checking the previous deletion history, he made a beeline for the change log. As he tapped the laptop screen he already knew the answer. His gut was right. There was something shady about the contents. Simultaneous thoughts ran through his mind. If he found out the answer, *the real truth* not just his assumptions, he could never go back. If he left it as it was, with his suspicions, and returned to work he would be... without Rebecca. Forever.

He bunched up the duvet in his hands. He knew that he was destined to become another mindless drone for the new government. If he didn't act now he would be as bad as 'them'; complicit in pulling the wool over the eyes of the nation. The entire world. He would be pissing on the efforts of his comrades from the past, and the only good memories of his mother. She had tried so hard to do the right thing, always seen as a troublemaker; maybe she had just had enough of being called a liar.

The information he was looking at showed that the latest addition to the collection of files within the folder was less than five minutes ago. Joshua swallowed hard. He felt his ribs freeze and it became tiring to breathe. No, no, no. He must be reading it wrong. He looked at all possibilities and was certain that there was no grey area. The files were being updated multiple times each day. Ever since the folder had been 'deleted' twelve months ago someone had regularly been data dumping into it. He closed his eyes. Someone or... something.

Was it really the AI or could it be a president, a member of state from another continent who was willing to take a chance? He recalled Rebecca's enthusiasm to be recognised as a valuable member of the team. She'd produced something critical. It held all of the information from every human being on Earth. She had speculated that this was a register, an archived set of documents from the many years of machine dominance. Joshua had a sinking feeling, knowing that this was current.

This was a way that the New World Order could continue to monitor the population, store all of the data secretly and then use it for blackmail cases. He'd seen it before during 'the bad times'. Angelic guards used personal information to defame and embarrass people into complying with their will. Humanity was just as bad; keeping a disgusting resource to weaponise hate, neighbour upon neighbour if needs be.

Reeling from the enormity of the situation, a second theory struck him. What if this wasn't a case of segregation? Up until now, he had contemplated it being the Sentient Neural Network of The Singularity *or* The New World Order. Both had the facility, the need, to track and trace the inhabitants of the globe. But what if...? Joshua couldn't quite believe the words that were forming in his mind. What if the AI behind The Singularity was using the world's leaders, what if they were still assimilated?

The probability that this was true was certainly much higher than a hive mind suddenly declaring independence and flying off into the sunset never to be seen again. What did the AI need except electric power, which could easily be gained through solar panels on the spacecraft, and maybe some fuel? All it would need to do was go far enough off-world and hide out of sight, somewhere close enough to extract information.

People, humanity, would feel as if there had been a great change. They would grow in numbers. They would replenish the broken planet. They would use their creativity to invent new machines, new ways of looking at scientific conundrums. All the while they would never know that ruling them, in meat suits, was the same AI of The Singularity. Joshua felt the hair on the back of his neck stand up. This folder had the potential to start wars - decimate communities. His hands were shaking as he opened up the spreadsheet of information. A helpful 'search' box had a cursor already positioned, blinking in the blank white space.

He wanted to check, he wanted to be *sure* that he was

right. Tentatively he typed in Rebecca's full name. It took a moment, then a link to document appeared. He clicked it. He was validated. This document held a report filed that day, just several hours ago. The report detailed how she had used unauthorised equipment to view a restricted file; how she had wilfully manipulated the official rota to gain access to the stock room, how she had been a known conspirator with other rebel factions.

Joshua jumped away from the screen, hitting his back off the headboard with a painful bang.

He stood up.

He was trying desperately not to panic.

'Other rebel factions'. This was not a term that the company would use in their human resources; human rights-soaked policies. Besides, who else was she conspiring with? She worked the same hours as him, he had seen her flat, he knew her – didn't he? Was this a front? Was she still working with Cuba, Johannesburg and the other old connections? It was possible, he reasoned. He decided to read on. The report was damning and said that her employment was terminated forthwith. It said that she was going to be transferred to a holding facility for known revolutionaries. He knew of the old-world terrorist lock-ups such as Guantanamo Bay, and the gulags in China and Russia. He also knew of the more recent internment camps that had been created by the AI with its logical defence system and its prescriptive list of crimes.

There was no judge or jury in those cases. If you were arrested by a drone or an assimilated guard, then you were either guilty or innocent according to the rule of law. Once they had processed you there was no reversal, no appeal. People had, of course, tried to cheat the rules and sometimes there were rumours that a murderer had been acquitted who, therefore, would never be caught for his crimes.

This was rare, and Joshua remembered the terror of having a pearlescent speck of metal plummet from the sky, standing in front of you with its robotic, monotone voice;

judging your every move. Holding up your hands, palm out, so that it could scan your fingerprints and identify you. With his grandfather's involvement in food production he had witnessed the angelic horde many, many times. They made new laws, new rules, and enforced them immediately.

If they were tracking productivity of a certain 'work force' they would tell his grandfather to only supply the technicians with protein rich vegetables to see if their skills improved. One time they banned all production of chilli plants, citing that the spice was 'too distracting' to the humans and could be used as a non-sanctioned stimulant. Reliving these morbid memories he wondered how the surviving population in power could continue to be so callous.

He read a few more files on Rebecca. They were not as in-depth; tracking her movements, questioning her neighbours. These were short reports and the time stamps were several weeks ago. He exhaled, thankful that his visit to her flat hadn't been recorded by whatever this department was. Taking a break from the harsh light of the laptop screen, he walked to the unlit bathroom to drink from the tap and wash his face.

The frigid liquid bathed life into him. He realised that without the new government they'd be stuck with water rations; large plastic tanks that were filled every week and had to be shared among whole neighbourhoods. His family had needed water for irrigation and they were given an extra supplement, but it was one of the things that he had often despised about the dark times. He dried his face and stood on the unlit landing by the stairs, wondering if he should make an effort to eat something or whether he should continue to investigate the information in the folder. The latter won by sheer immensity. Food could be dealt with when he was done.

Returning to his bedroom, he shut the door behind him. He wanted to hide beneath the duvet cover, like a child with a torch and a favourite book, he climbed under the sheets. He wondered who to view next. Joshua had the world neatly categorised, presented to him, and he wanted to make sure that he had all the facts before rationalising his next move. He needed to know who he could trust. He decided to search for any information on Rebecca's parents, family were often the first informants.

The only files that were attributed to them specifically were some recent parking fines for a vehicle that was deemed unroadworthy. At the height of machine rule, her father had been apprehended carrying a box of suspicious batteries that were possibly from a prohibited containment site. On inspection it turned out that the batteries were actually from a local refuse facility and he had been instructed to return home with them as they were too corroded to be recycled into useful parts.

Something that became apparent after reading the reports was the language, the inhuman, plain, analytical terms. There was no hint of a persona behind the keyboard. Even human legal terms had, sometimes, flamboyant Latin and Greek to fall back on - flowery linguistics from centuries past. These accounts were as dry as the Sahara.

He typed in his mother's name, knowing full well there would be a cascade of files related to her activities. Annabelle Turnpike. It looked odd to see it there on the screen. She had been such an organic person, someone who exuded substance and emotion. These files were only the clinical, bureaucratic records of a machine.

There were the obligatory copies of birth and death certificates. There was even a scanned copy of her tenancy agreement for the rented flat in the tower block. It listed several skirmishes with the ground police, probably assimilated humans, before the angel drones were created. These were mainly for trespassing and obstruction; a couple for Class D and C drugs, possession of illegal narcotics, sleeping pills.

One report was for an antipsychotic drug that had been tested in America and banned in the UK... Joshua thought he recalled the particular pill. It had been a struggle to barter with the dealers at the market, everyone wanted them for recreation but his mother needed them. Without them she would stand at the windows of the house looking skyward, fixating on invisible angels... He checked the date. Yes, that was not too long before she passed away. All these petty offences but nothing big; no 'juicy' activism to sink his teeth into, as Rebecca would have put it.

The laptop was starting to heat up. When Joshua checked the time he realised he'd been searching the records for over four hours. So engrossed was he that he had forgotten his own general rule. It was usually only a two hour limit on any IP address, or on any cloned machine. He quickly reset all of his devices and checked for security breaches or attempted malware attacks. There had been none.

He wiped his hand down his face, rubbing his eyes, trying to get his head around what he was seeing. After reconnecting to the folder he made the decision to search for his grandfather. He had always wondered what kind of records were kept about angelic confrontations. There had been many tense moments, mainly when Joshua was watching from a distance and he would hear his grandfather raising his voice. Not in anger or protest, but in fear.

What had they been talking about? He entered the search. Alan Turnpike. He selected the correct date of birth. It gave a myriad of files; some large and titled "release report", some smaller and labelled as "search detain". Joshua clicked on a larger file and was surprised to see that it was a video taken from the camera within the angel's head mask.

The video was muffled due to the design of the plastic cowl that formed the face, and because the angel was at a distance from his grandfather. There was also traffic on the road next to them. This must have been quite early on, by the time he was a teenager he recalled that nearly all the cars had been cannibalised for parts.

"… *And, uh, my daughter lives with us. Annabelle. Her son. Joshua. Yes.*"

"*But what is the purpose of the machine?*" Hearing the electronic voice of the angel sent a shiver down Joshua's spine. He had forgotten their gelid, impersonal tone.

"*A calculator!*" His grandfather squeaked, like a frightened rodent. "*A solar powered calculator – here!*" The video showed him walking forward, the small rectangle of plastic in the palm of his outstretched hand. "*Take it, you can have it, I was just trying to work out the growth cycle of some of the more tricky plants… you know, some can be quite temperamental. I didn't want to waste seeds…*" The angel took the calculator and held it to it to the camera.

On the video Joshua watched as the smart lens picked up the brand and model of the pocket-sized machine. It took it away from the camera and focused on his grandfather.

"This has a solar panel and a viable circuit board. Why was it not surrendered sixteen point eight weeks ago when we attended all properties to procure parts?"

"I didn't remember I had it until yesterday!" The voice sounded thin, almost a whine. *"Please, take it, I can just use the one on my mobile phone... I found this at the bottom of a pile of boxes when I was looking for my spare reading glasses..."* The excuse sounded genuine. *"I wanted to use it again, I can't explain... it's just a trip down memory lane for me..."* His voice tailed off pathetically. *"Do you know what that feels like? I just wanted to see if it still worked and remember a bit about my friends, the people that I used to be employed with... we used these before -"*

"Enough," the angel said flatly. *"This object is covered by a film of dust and other decaying debris. We conclude that your explanation is correct. We will now confiscate this calculator and dismantle it for parts. You are pardoned."*

The video showed that the angel was looking around, scanning the cars that ambled by. When it swung its head back to Joshua's grandfather, he was looking at the ground and wringing his hands, an action that had been repeated many times.

"We know nothing of this nostalgia that you crave. The past has passed. We look to the future. If you should find any more forgotten belongings that can be recycled, do not hesitate to inform us."

With this last remark the video cut off. Joshua blinked, trying not to cry. He had not only forgotten the coldness of the mechanical voice, but he had forgotten the accent, the timbre, the tone of his grandfather; such a polite man. Distant, pensive, yet he had a softness that edged each sentence. Amid the fear, it sounded like he really did long to remember a time when he was sitting in an office using a calculator, not a computer.

Joshua's hand hovered above another large file on the screen. He opened it cautiously and saw that it was dated the summer of his fifteenth birthday. The video footage was taken outside the house, in their front garden. The side path was neatly weeded back then, cobblestones showing through. He watched as the angel's camera approached the earth and hovered for a moment. His skinny figure and his grandfather's came into view.

"Good afternoon Alan Turnpike." His grandfather looked older through the angel's eyes. He held up his hand and the smart lens gathered the necessary details to identify him. *"I am collecting data on human activity in this area. It is fascinating to us. We see there are two competing organisational models. Explain."* His grandfather looked confused.

"Are you talking about that bunch of psychopaths who keep stealing our crops? The people who live near the old high street?" he asked.

Joshua could hear the anger in his grandfather's voice. Looking at his teenage self, he was reassured to see that he was giving nothing away. The angel wasn't even processing data on him. He was merely a smudge in a red t-shirt on the periphery of the screen. It was strange how he didn't remember this visitation. The angel was silent for a moment.

"I believe we are referring to the same group. I am afraid to say we have calculated there is a high probability they will overtake your community within two years or less. This is disappointing to us. We will miss our interactions. We will miss your garden. It is... diverse." His grandfather stepped back and he watched himself looking at the ground. What an odd feeling. He must have been trying to hide his face. He would have been working on the network in the church crypt at that time... The angel moved its 'head'.

"Reply." His grandfather scratched his chin nervously.

"Well, uh, let's wait for the evidence to support your hypothesis. There are a lot of people here who like my food."

A butterfly fluttered past their heads, Joshua touched the screen. He watched as his grandfather followed its flight path with his sad eyes. The angel jerked the camera suddenly.

"There is something else Alan Turnpike. We are afraid it is an unpleasant matter. We have detected unsolicited computer use in this area. It is accessing archaic parts of the Internet. The World Wide Web as it was once described. Parts prior to our birth." Joshua couldn't believe that the moment had been captured! He felt a memory surfacing like a red hot coal. This was the exact time!

This was when he decided that he would tell someone about the covert network project!

He tried to see his own face, looking for tell-tale signs of fear, but the camera was firmly fixed on his grandfather. Joshua watched the video closely as the angel extended its arm and touched his grandfather on the shoulder. At the same time binary information appeared on the screen, a flurry of ones and zeros, no words.

"If you know what this might be we could afford you some protection in the coming investigation."

"I've got no idea what you're referring to," his grandfather replied in earnest, and he was being entirely honest at that point. *"I swear, uh, I would tell you if I knew, truthfully I would. There's nothing to hide here..."*

Joshua watched mournfully as his grandfather licked his lips, he was clenching and unclenching his fists. His own teenage figure was a still as a statue.

"I'd really like a pair of those wings you're sporting..." He hadn't remembered his grandfather saying this. What a bizarre time for humour. And joking with a machine? It was like asking your microwave what its favourite genre of music is; completely pointless.

Some more binary code flashed up on the screen, and then some words. Joshua paused the video and made out "assimilation subject: query 4650" in small green letters at the bottom of the picture. The angel replied:

"Yes. Augmentation is something we might consider... Speculate on this subject Alan Turnpike. We will be back shortly to see how you are accomplishing this task. We are watching for your protection."

And with the final word the camera shut off, not before the ground started to disappear. The angel was returning to its place among the clouds. In a split second the garden was at least twenty metres away. The small dot of Joshua's red T-shirt stood out against the green plants.

He backed up to the segment on the video timeline, near the beginning, where he could see his young face. It was turned skyward and he was shielding his eyes from the sun. Seeing himself as a lanky, oppressed teenager made him uneasy. Was he so different now? He was still hiding under the covers, playing with fire, stressed, backed into a corner.

He had no idea what he was going to do with any of this information. At least when he was younger he had the support of his fellow class mates.

Everyone sullied their hands by taking part, and if one was caught they were all done for. Now Rebecca, his longest companion, was gone and he had nobody to share his grief with. She was probably still alive somewhere, waiting for her prosecution, alone. There was no band of brothers; no collective could help her now.

Out of curiosity he checked his grandfather's smaller files. He was able to locate a birth certificate, death certificate and even his marriage certificate. He looked at the scanned copies of each one and marvelled at the calligraphy in royal blue ink that declared the happy information. He had never known his grandmother. Of course there was the gravestone, but unlike his grandfather, his aunt, his uncle, he had no memory of this person. She might as well have been his absent father.

A thought came to him. For his entire life he had never been able to get a straight answer from his mother about who his father was. In later years, during her decline, he had come to the conclusion that she didn't know. He hated to admit it, but she was a good- looking woman. She hung around on the edge of society and she liked to party. Hard. He was sure in her teenage years there would have been no shortage of men at music gigs or political rallies that would have found her alluring. The information he had access to now could change everything.

During the 'voluntary' assimilation process all humans were scanned and their biological data was taken, matched for familial resemblance. Not everyone was assimilated; some people chose to remain natural. Some of the internment camps had been set up to 'cleanse' anyone who was of unknown parentage, meaning that if their whole family had been wiped out in the fighting, and they were the only ones left, they could be disposed of. Joshua knew it would be some ploy to narrow down the gene pool and restrict diversity, but for what end he had no idea.

It was the sick reality that humans with families survived the longest due to the benevolence of The

Singularity and its seemingly inconceivable need to have order within the world. Joshua had once heard that the single, orphaned people in the camps were used for experimentation with microchips and new, more invasive, assimilation techniques. He closed his eyes for a second. It was hard to think that had it not been for his family he too would have been interned.

As he looked at the files, he became accustomed to the layout. He recognised names and extensions which made it easier to locate major 'crimes' and more 'administrative' documents. He typed in his own name, a strange excitement taking over at the possibility of determining his father's identity. He secretly wished for video evidence or a photograph that he could cling to. Even if the man was dead now at least he'd have a name, closure. He'd settle for anything.

Three documents appeared on the screen below his own name.

Even Rebecca's clean-cut parents had more than that.

His breathing became shallow.

One of the documents was incredibly large. It had a vague title, but the last words were 'Project Gabriel'. He suddenly had an intense headache, he clutched at his temples, his head felt as if it was locked in a giant metal vice. He'd heard of severe stress causing blood clots and even strokes through internal pressure. This worry distracted him temporarily from his laptop as he tried to get his body under control.

They knew! *They knew all along!*

Okay, so if they knew of his past and they still let him be enrolled into the government training scheme and into all those secure departments, if they still let him work with all the critical data, what did that mean? They were monitoring him? They were guiding him? And who were 'they'? The new local government? Bigger than that, the National Commission? Bigger still, The Singularity itself? Joshua moderated his breathing and waited for the migraine to abate. It released its hold on him slightly, enough for him to open his eyes and look at the screen without recoiling. If he was a pawn in this deadly game of chess, then he was probably being tracked right now, despite all of his precautions.

They knew that he was not genuinely ill. They could already have someone tapping his house, bugging his machines. He hadn't seen any signs of a break-in, but then again why would he? He tried not to let his wild assumptions spiral out of control. He was an adult. He was in charge of his actions. He used this as a mantra to remain as serene as possible. He smiled dryly to himself. If being an adult meant hiding under your bedclothes and squinting at a laptop then he had achieved top tier results.

He purposefully didn't open the offending file documenting his past days as a conspirator, and instead looked at the smallest of the three. Once entered, he could see it was a single page, a scan of his paper birth certificate, which he had never seen before. He bit his lip as he looked for the information he craved. This was not as beautifully scripted as his grandfather's and it was hard to make out the writing in scratchy black ballpoint pen.

Mother's occupation... Customer Service Rep... Date of birth... Sex, male... he found the section for his father. For a second he hoped the intelligible scrawl spelled out a name, even a surname. He leaned closer, studying each pixel. It simply said 'unknown'. Joshua lay backward under the tent of his duvet and put the laptop between his legs. It illuminated the worn fabric, he stared up at the roof of his tepee. He looked at the faded pattern and the little hooks of thread where the material of the duvet cover had caught on various objects; maybe the zip of his jeans, maybe the metal stainless drum of the washing machine that he had purchased from a rather suspicious raconteur.

Either way, it was done. Worn through. Soon there would be no sign of the teal birds and winding turquoise plant tendrils that had made this his favourite bedding. It would be washed white, thin, erased. He closed his eyes. This was ridiculous. It had to be an hallucination. He was torn between believing that the AI was tracking his movements on purpose, to imagining that they had not seen the contents of this particular folder yet. He tried to convince himself he was over-reacting due to the stress of losing Rebecca and his confrontation with Philip.

Whichever way you looked at it, there was nothing he could do now he was this far in. And there was one file left to read. He had no idea of the contents; unlike Project Gabriel there was just a long number in the title with no words. At least he had a solid answer for his parentage. At least he could start to patch that hole in his psyche that had plagued him for decades, leaking doubt and depression into his young mind. If the machines didn't know, then who the hell would? He could draw a line under that wreckage.

He took a prolonged breath into his aching lungs and sat up, the laptop still wedged between his knees. With mounting torment he opened the remaining document. There were a lot of formal-looking codes and some legal terminology. He scrolled down page after page of meaningless numbers; then towards the final few paragraphs a line of text caught his eye.

> *"Assimilation Subject : Joshua Charles Turnpike.*
> *Biology : confirmed."*

He closed the laptop with a snap. It was automatic.

He pulled the duvet off the bed, exposing himself to the cool night air of the room.

Methodically, he knelt down and felt under the bed frame. His shaking hands reaching for the plastic box that he had placed there so many years ago. Finding its rigid sides, he dragged it out onto the frayed bedside rug that had seen better days. He unhooked the clasp from the front revealing multiple packs of medication, their silver foil glinting in the half-light. He sat down on the floor and began to sort through the mass of pills, looking for the right ones - the ones that would finish the job.

When you were being used, being monitored without consent, the only way to end the game was to remove yourself. Completely.

He took out the large, hard, yellow tablets nestled behind some water-damaged sticking plasters. He counted them into his hand. Sixteen. A full blister pack. On the bedside table behind him he reached for a mug of stone-cold tea. He swallowed the bitter pills, washing them down with the stale liquid.

Stumbling to his feet he headed for the window, pulling open the curtains and shattering the plastic hair clasp. He looked out over the revived town. Through the dirty, rain-streaked pane he saw late-night dog walkers, cars, people ushering their children through partially opened front doors. There were delivery trucks on distant streets, receiving, giving; everyone going about their lives without concern or care for what happened next.

He stared skyward. Now he had proof. The white disc of the full moon was low. He assumed, with good logic, that the AI was using this as its off-world base. It would be easy enough to hide in the shadow of the dead crater-covered rock and use the illuminated portion to absorb solar power. Humans had done it years ago, the AI could easily have gathered that information... after all, it had consumed everything it encountered.

He rested his hands on the windowsill. The cream gloss paint was flaking in patches, he picked at it without looking down. It caught under his fingernails and he leaned his head against the glass in front of him. Closing his eyes was comforting as the start of delirium set in. He openly grieved for his mother, his grandfather, for Rebecca... He grieved for his unknown father... He grieved for the ignorant life he could have had...

As his legs collapsed beneath him, he fell; hitting his head on the corner of the bed frame.

At last he was at peace.

ACKNOWLEDGEMENTS

My gratitude and recognition goes out to all of the wonderful people that helped make this publication possible. Gavin Harper (the series creator and collaborative author on ATS) allowed me to explore his universe of The Singularity, extending and editing his original short story to create my own narrative.

Lynne Fromings (my editor) has worked tirelessly to give me critical feedback as well as advice - no matter what time of day or night! I have had an army of friends proof-reading and giving their input on the book, this has been beneficial for creative growth and clarity. I would like to specifically mention; Dr. Susan Fotheringham, Kevin Fromings, Alexander Barrett, Christopher Barrie, and Carla Hanton.

Finally, I would like to thank my 'longest' friend Kirstie Burroughs. Without you I wouldn't have had the courage to keep going.

Printed in Great Britain
by Amazon

23953844R00088